Contents

WHEN SINDY'S FRIEND, JO, LEFT "IN VOGUE," THE BIG FASHION HOUSE, TO SET UP ON HER OWN, SHE HAD VERY LITTLE MONEY TO SPEND ON PUBLICITY FOR THE SKI WEAR SINDY HAD DESIGNED FOR HER. IT WAS SINDY'S IDEA TO USE A SMALL STUDIO AND ARTIFICIAL SNOW TO KEEP COSTS DOWN. THE RESULTS WERE EVEN BETTER THAN SHE HAD EXPECTED, BUT WHEN SHE TOOK THE FIRST PROOFS TO SHOW TO HER FRIEND...
MARK WINTERTON!
HELLO, SINDY! MEET MY NEW PUBLICITY CHIEF!
Sindy's Snow Maidens
I THOUGHT YOU WERE WELL IN OVER AT "IN VOGUE"!
I WAS UNTIL I FELL OUT WITH THE BOSS! YOU KNOW AS WELL AS I DO WHAT LYDIA STEINER CAN BE LIKE!
I HOPE YOU DON'T THINK MARK IS TREADING ON YOUR TOES! NOW HE IS TAKING OVER THE PUBLICITY, YOU CAN GET BACK TO DESIGNING THE BEACH WEAR! I REALLY AM GRATEFUL FOR ALL YOU HAVE DONE, SINDY!
JO WAS TELLING ME HOW YOU PUT OFF YOUR WINTER BREAK TO HELP OUT, SINDY!
YOU CAN TROT OFF AND ENJOY YOURSELF NOW! I BELIEVE THE BAHAMAS IS LOVELY AT THIS TIME OF YEAR! IT SHOULD GIVE YOU LOTS OF INSPIRATION FOR YOUR BEACHWEAR COLLECTION!
WE'LL LOOK AT THESE LATER, SINDY! OFF YOU GO AND HAVE FUN!
I HOPE YOU KNOW WHAT YOU ARE DOING, JO! I WOULDN'T TRUST HIM ANY FARTHER THAN I COULD THROW HIM!

NOT FOR SINDY THE SUNNY BAHAMAS NOR THE FASHIONABLE SKI RESORTS. SHE STAYED AT AN INN IN A SMALL SWISS VILLAGE TUCKED AWAY IN THE ALPS WHERE SHE COULD SKI AWAY FROM THE CROWDED SLOPES AND SPEND HER EVENINGS QUIETLY INSTEAD OF AT PARTIES. SINDY ENJOYED PARTIES, BUT THERE WERE TIMES WHEN SHE PREFERRED TO BE ON HER OWN...
PHEW! THAT WAS GREAT! I'LL JUST GET MY BREATH BACK AND GO AND GET SOME LUNCH!
LOOKS AS IF SOMEONE ELSE IS STOPPING FOR LUNCH!
INN.
SINDY WAS IN FOR A SURPRISE WHEN SHE ENTERED THE INN...
SINDY!
HOW LOVELY TO SEE YOU!
SUE AND PRU! WHAT ARE YOU DOING HERE?
SUE AND PRU WERE TWO TOP MODELS MUCH IN DEMAND IN THE FASHION WORLD...
WE GOT A BIT BORED HANGING AROUND THE RESORT! WE'RE NOT WHAT YOU MIGHT CALL WINTER SPORTY SORTS!
WE PINCHED MARK'S CAR WHEN HE WASN'T LOOKING TO GO FOR A SPIN AND ENDED UP HERE.
MARK'S CAR? YOU MEAN MARK WINTERTON?
ACTUALLY IT ISN'T HIS! HE IS ONLY HIRING IT WHILE WE'RE IN VERMITZ! WE'RE NOT HERE FOR PLEASURE, SINDY! WE'RE HERE ON A JOB!
YOU COULD FOOL ME! I DON'T KNOW WHEN I'VE LIVED IT UP SO MUCH! IT'S BEEN QUITE A JUNKET! I'D HATE TO BE PAYING FOR IT!

POOR JO!
WE'VE JUST TIME FOR SOME DESSERT AND THEN WE'LL HAVE TO GO!
MARK'LL WANT HIS CAR TO MEET LYDIA AT THE AIRPORT!
LYDIA STEINER? IS SHE COMING HERE?
IF SHE IS THE ONE WHO IS SPLASHING OUT SHE MIGHT AS WELL JOIN IN THE FUN!
RUMOUR HAS IT THEY MIGHT ANNOUNCE THEIR MARRIAGE AT A PARTY TOMORROW NIGHT! WHY DON'T YOU COME OVER? IT COULD BE WHY MARK IS SPENDING HER MONEY AS THOUGH IT WERE GOING OUT OF FASHION!
SINDY WATCHED THE LARGE CAR DEPART...
LOVELY TO SEE YOU, SINDY! DO TRY TO GET OVER TOMORROW NIGHT!
I THINK I'D BETTER LET JO KNOW WHAT IS GOING ON!
SINDY INTENDED TO TELEPHONE JO AS SOON AS THE GIRLS HAD LEFT...
THE TELEPHONES ARE OUT OF ORDER, MISS SINDY! THERE HAS BEEN AN AVALANCHE IN THE VALLEY! ALL THE VILLAGES HAVE BEEN CUT OFF!
WHERE IS THE NEAREST TELEPHONE THEN?
VERMITZ! THE QUICKEST WAY THERE IS TO SKI, BUT IT WILL BE DARK BEFORE YOU GET THERE!
IS THERE NO OTHER FORM OF TRANSPORT?

IT IS STARTING TO SNOW! THERE HAS BEEN A HEAVY FALL BETWEEN HERE AND VERMITZ. THE ROADS WILL BE BLOCKED BEFORE YOU CAN GET THERE!
BUT I MUST GET IN TOUCH WITH MY FRIEND IN ENGLAND!
TOMORROW I SET OUT AT FIRST LIGHT TO SKI OVER TO VERMITZ! YOU GIVE ME THE MESSAGE, I SEND IT FOR YOU!
THANKS, BUT I WANT TO SPEAK TO HER MYSELF! HAVE YOU ANY OBJECTION IF I COME WITH YOU?
AND AT FIRST LIGHT THE FOLLOWING MORNING...
I DID NOT KNOW THAT YOU WERE A PHOTOGRAPHER, WILLI!
JA! I TAKE PICTURES OF THE TOURISTS ON THE SKI SLOPES! IT IS A LIVING! OFTEN I TELL LISA, MY GIRL, THAT MAYBE ONE DAY I HIT THE BIG TIME!
MAYBE YOU LIKE TO MEET LISA! HER VILLAGE IS IN THAT DIRECTION! I ALWAYS CALL IN AND SEE HER EACH MORNING! IT IS ONLY TEN MINUTES SKIING FROM HERE!
THANKS! BUT IT IS REALLY IMPORTANT THAT I GET ON! IF YOU COULD POINT ME IN THE RIGHT DIRECTION I'LL GO ON ALONE!
SINDY HAD SKIED SOME DISTANCE WHEN SHE STOPPED TO ADJUST ONE OF HER SKI STRAPS...
WELL! WELL! WELL! IF IT ISN'T SINDY! JUST THE PERSON I WAS COMING TO SEE!
HOW UNFORTUNATE FOR YOU THAT YOUR FRIENDS DECIDED TO BORROW MY CAR!
MARK WINTERTON!

I'M AFRAID THEY TALK TOO MUCH! I MUST MAKE SURE THAT YOU DON'T!
YOU COULDN'T HAVE CHOSEN A BETTER SPOT TO STOP! IDEAL FOR A NASTY SKIING ACCIDENT, DON'T YOU THINK?

SINDY DID NOT STOP TO THINK...
SO THAT'S HOW YOU INTEND TO SILENCE ME!
THE CHASE WAS ON...

I CAN'T KEEP THIS UP MUCH LONGER!

IN HER HASTE TO GET AWAY, SINDY LOST ALL SENSE OF DIRECTION...
THEN SINDY SAW THE DISTANT FIGURES, AND SO DID HER PURSUER...
HELP ME! HELP ME!
I'D BETTER GET OUT OF HERE FAST!

MY GOODNESS! THEY'RE SCULPTED OUT OF SNOW!

BY THE TIME SINDY FOUND HER WAY BACK TO THE VILLAGE THE TELEPHONES WERE WORKING AGAIN. IT WAS A VERY SHATTERED JO WHO SINDY MET AT THE AIRPORT THAT EVENING...

I CHECKED AS SOON AS I GOT YOUR CALL, SINDY! HAVE I BEEN TAKEN TO THE CLEANERS!

I GOT ON TO THE POLICE AS QUICKLY AS I COULD, BUT THE BIRDS HAD FLOWN! THE CAR HE HIRED IS OUTSIDE THE AIRPORT! YOU'VE PAID FOR IT SO I SUGGEST WE USE IT!

IN THEIR HASTE TO DEPART, MARK WINTERTON'S PARTY HAD LEFT SINDY'S CREATIONS BEHIND. THE HOTEL MANAGEMENT WOULD NOT RELEASE THEM UNTIL SOMEBODY PAID THE BILL...
THERE IS NO WAY YOU GET THOSE CLOTHES UNTIL SOMEBODY PAYS THE BILL!
DON'T LOOK AT ME! I'M JUST ABOUT BANKRUPT!
THERE COULD BE A WAY!

...AND IF WE MODELLED THE CLOTHES WITH YOUR HOTEL IN THE BACKGROUND, THINK OF ALL THE PUBLICITY YOU'D BE GETTING IN ALL THE TOP FASHION MAGAZINES!
JA! I AM THINKING, AND THE MORE I AM THINKING THE MORE I AM LIKING!

YOU AND YOUR BRIGHT IDEAS, SINDY! I CAN'T AFFORD TO PAY ANY MODELS, OR A PHOTOGRAPHER!
REMEMBER THOSE SNOW STATUES I TOLD YOU ABOUT THAT SAVED ME FROM WINTERTON? IF WE CAN FIND OUT WHO MADE THEM, THEY MIGHT JUST SAVE YOU, TOO! I THINK I CAN FIND A PHOTOGRAPHER! HE MIGHT BE AT THE INN!

WILLI WAS...
YOU MEAN YOU KNOW WHO MADE THOSE SCULPTURES IN SNOW?
I OUGHT TO! AS SOON AS WE HAVE MADE ENOUGH MONEY SHE WILL BE MY WIFE! TOMORROW WE GO OVER AND SEE LISA! I AM SURE SHE WILL BE HAPPY TO TAKE TIME OFF FROM DECORATING CUCKOO CLOCKS!
LISA WAS ONLY TOO HAPPY TO OBLIGE. HER SNOW MAIDENS IN SKI CLOTHES APPEARED ON THE SKI SLOPES, ON THE SKI LIFTS, OUTSIDE THE HOTEL, EVEN UP AT THE BAR...
WHEN SINDY AND JO SAW THE PROOFS, JO KNEW SHE WAS ON TO A WINNER...
THE GLOSSIES WILL BE FALLING OVER BACKWARDS TO GET THESE! SINDY, I THINK I CAN SAFELY SAY THAT I'M STILL IN BUSINESS!
IN THAT CASE I THINK A LITTLE CELEBRATION IS CALLED FOR, AND IF YOU LET ME HAVE BIG BLOW-UPS OF THE PICTURES FOR THE HOTEL WALLS, YOU MAY HAVE ALL YOUR SKI CLOTHES BACK!
LATER, BACK AT THE INN...
THANK YOU WILLI AND LISA! I WANT YOU BOTH OVER FOR MY NEXT ASSIGNMENT! MEAN-TIME HOW CAN I PAY YOU FOR WHAT YOU'VE BOTH DONE?
I'LL SETTLE FOR A SKI SUIT!
I WOULD LIKE SINDY TO POSE FOR ME BEFORE SHE LEAVES, SO MAYBE I MAKE MY SNOW MAIDENS LOOK EVEN BETTER!
WHAT OUT IN THE SNOW?

NO! IN MY WARM STUDIO! FATHER HAS PROMISED THAT IF I BECOME SUCCESSFUL AS A SCULPTRESS, HE'LL LET ME OFF DECORATING CUCKOO CLOCKS!

WHEN SINDY RETURNED FROM HER WINTER HOLIDAY AND WALKED INTO JO'S OFFICE, SHE GOT QUITE A SHOCK...
LYDIA STEINER! WHAT NOW?
HELLO, SINDY! I AM HERE TO APOLOGISE FOR MARK'S BEHAVIOUR. I ASSURE YOU THAT I DID NOT PUT HIM UP TO IT! I'M AFRAID THE FOOL BELIEVED ME WHEN I SAID THAT I WOULD MARRY HIM WHEN JO WENT OUT OF BUSINESS... I MEANT NEVER!

THEN WHY DID YOU LEAVE IN SUCH A HURRY WITH HIM?

I DID NOT! I ONLY ARRIVED IN VERMITZ YESTERDAY! I HAD BEEN ON BUSINESS IN BERNE! I WENT TO SEE THE SNOW MAIDENS THAT EVERYONE WAS TALKING ABOUT! THE HOTEL MANAGER TOLD ME HOW THEY CAME TO BE THERE! I MUST CONGRATULATE THE PAIR OF YOU!

NOT ME! JUST SINDY... SHE'S THE ONE WITH THE BRIGHT IDEAS!

I'LL BE SENDING YOU A CHEQUE TO PAY FOR ALL HIS DEBTS!
HEAR THAT, SINDY? WHERE WOULD I BE BUT FOR YOU?
WHERE WOULD I BE BUT FOR THOSE SNOW MAIDENS?

Sindy's Pop Gossip

Wham!:

Whilst Andy and George of 'Wham!' are hard workers and seem never to be out of the charts, they do love their holidays. "We're not the kind of people who are all work and no play," says Andy. "So far we've been taking breaks in Spain, Florida and Hawaii and George went to Cyprus. The first thing we do is rent a car or bike or some kind of transport and then go exploring. You won't find us wasting time sunbathing." But there is one thing that Andy wishes he could have tried and that is being a racing car driver. "I just love the excitment of the sport," he says.

Frankie Goes to Hollywood:

Now that 'Frankie Goes Hollywood' are world famous they have to trave lot in 'planes. "And what w hate most is flying," they say. "When we went to New York we steeled our nerves and went for a tour of the city in a helicopter. It was exciting but darting between these skyscrapers at speed was worse than any airline trip!"

Paul Young:

If you want to become a pop singer then you've got to start early and use any audience that you can find. At least that seems to be the message that Paul Young is ready to stand by. "When I was a kid, I can remember the first concert I did," he laughs. "It was on top of a double decker bus. I was travelling with my Mum when I suddenly stood up and sang to all the people. She was so embarrassed but I had a great time." Be interesting to know if any of those passengers realise just how far he's come since that impromptu debut!

Alison Moyet:

That super powerful sing Alison Moyet, known to friends as, Alf, knows exactly what to do when sh wants some peace and quiet and someone to talk to. She goes and chats with chickens.

She keeps some in the back garden of her home and confesses that going out and talking to them helps her to concentrate more. It also means some tasty eggs for breakfast!

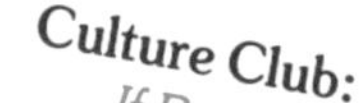

Culture Club:

If Boy George attracts the attention because of his clothes and voice, then it is Jon Moss, who is the group's pin up. But whilst he is a millionaire now, he once knew the good life and gave it up for a life of poverty. "We had servants and all the trimmings at home when I grew up," he says. "My Dad wanted me to be a lawyer or something like that. But I gave up the chauffeur driven cars for the life of a pop star and really had to scramble around for enough money for the next meal." Paid off, though, didn't it!

Spandau Ballet:

Tony Hadley, lead singer with the group, 'Spandau Ballet', *has a lot of interests to pursue when he isn't making records or touring the world. "One of them is horse riding," he says. "There's nothing I like better than to be able to go out into the country on horseback. I keep a horse at a special stable and often enter for competitions. They're not major events yet, but I do have a lot of fun competing." He also says that he'd like to be able to do acting some day so perhaps he'll be able to put his riding skills to use in a film!*

Duran Duran:

Making videos for their records in exotic locations might look fun for the guys of 'Duran Duran' *but it also has some nervous moments.*

"When we were in Sri Lanka filming," they say, "we were walking along the road when we suddenly turned round and saw this elephant following us. Luckily someone was riding him, but it was certainly a surprise.

"But even that was surpassed when we went to have a drink at a cafe. A man sat down next to us with a basket and when he opened it this huge snake popped out. It really scared us!" Sounds like the group live dangerously.

Prince:

Prince must be one of the most mysterious and yet exciting performers in the pop world, with the enormous success of his film and album, 'Purple Rain' behind him. Now he threatens Michael Jackson's crown as the leading pop star in the world. But whilst he might be a multi-millionaire there was a time when he was so poor that he used to sleep on friends' floors for the night. Now he can probably afford a string of houses around the world!

Sindy's Puzzle Pages

SEASIDE SCENE

I do like a day at the seaside and in particular a spot of water skiing, as you can see. Hmm. The lovely warm sun, the sea and the sand. Sun, sea, sand. That gives me an idea for a puzzle. How many other things can you find in this picture beginning with the letter 'S', and don't include me in your list!

PLACE THE PLACES

As you know I very often jet around to various parts of the world on one assignment or another. Here on the indicator board are just a few of the places I've visited. Can you unravel the names?

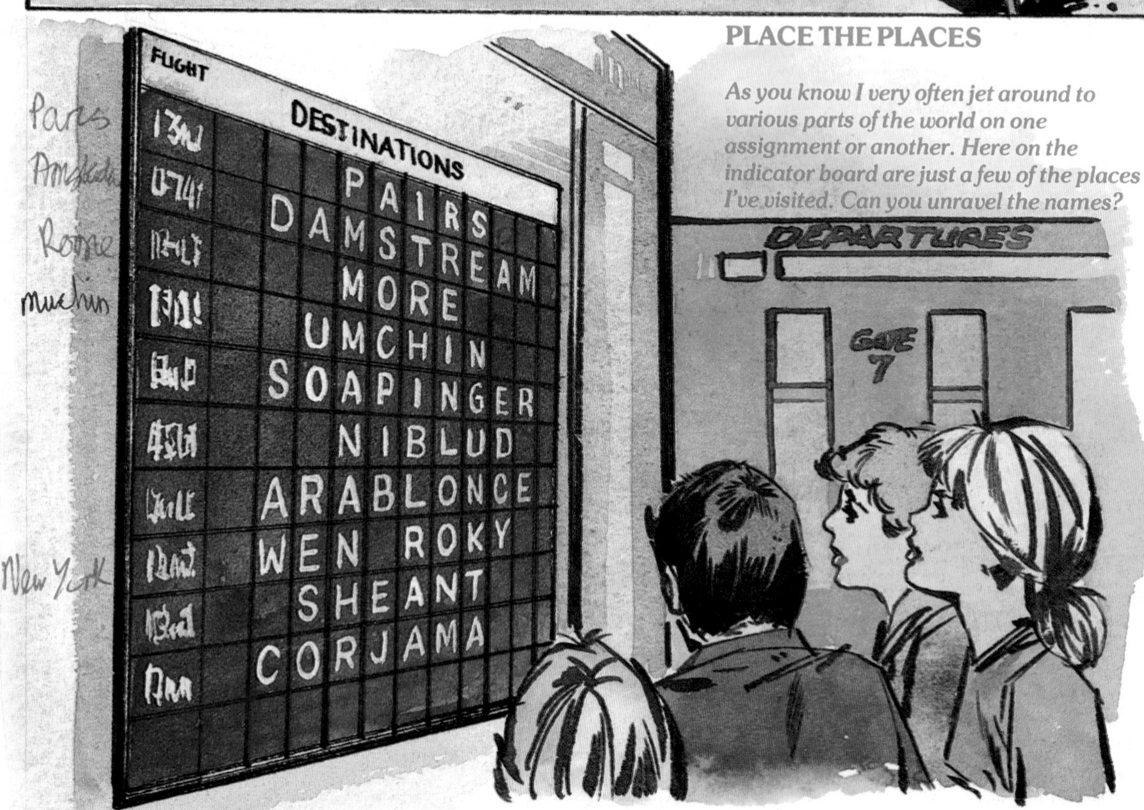

Hi! Do you like doing puzzles? I do. I think they're great fun. I thought you might like to test your skill and observation powers with these 4 teasers. The answers are on page 63 — but no peeping!

ALL ALIKE? NOT QUITE!

Shown below are 4 pictures of me in one of my favourite outfits. They may all look alike, but only 2 are. Can you spot which ones?

WHICH HORSE IS THE BIGGEST?

Out for a hike in the country the other day I saw 3 of my friends enjoying a trek, each riding her favourite horse. Can you tell which horse is the biggest? Is it Pam's in the front, Jill's in the middle or Pat's at the back?

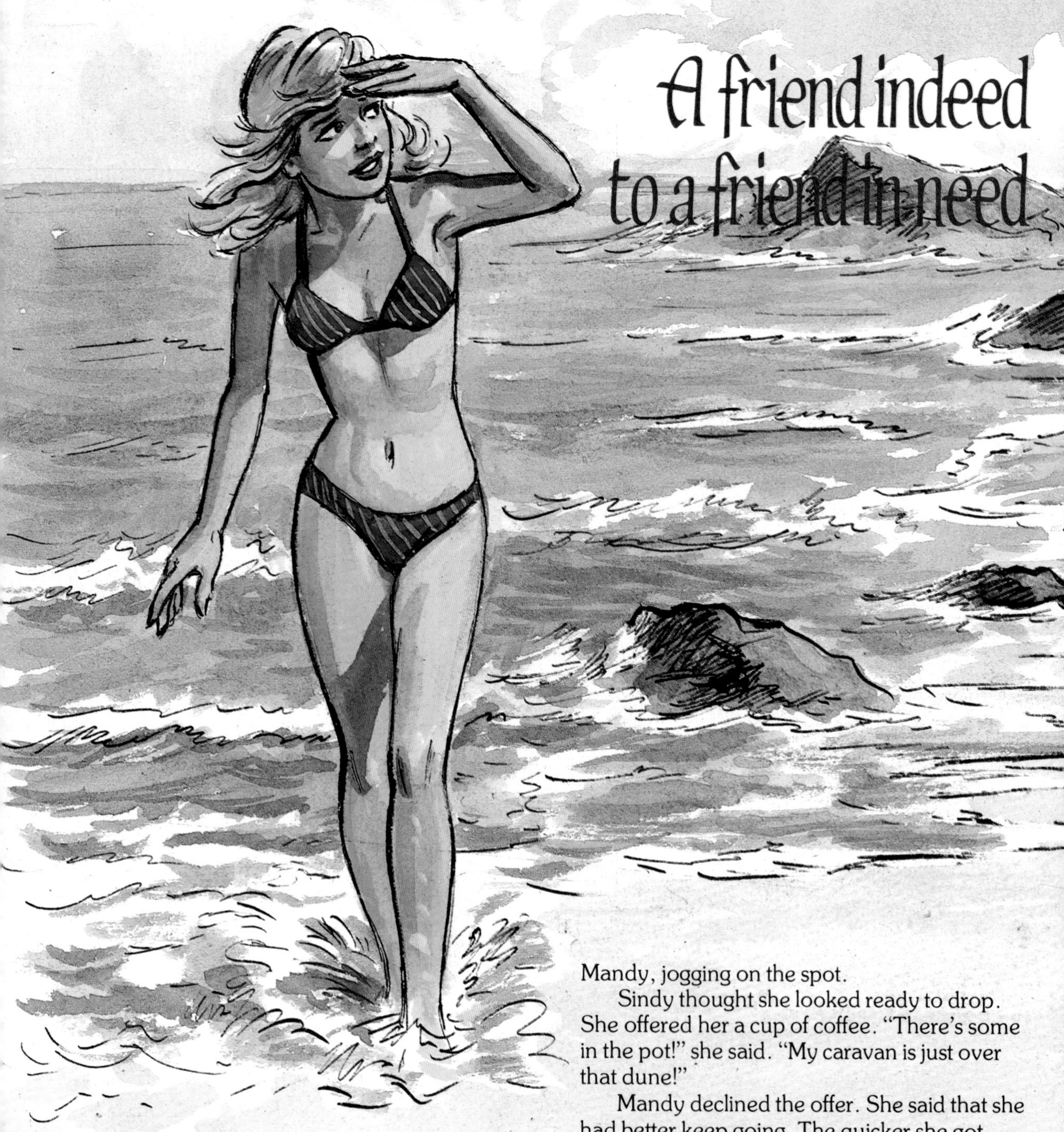

A friend indeed to a friend in need

Sindy had been very busy and was now taking a well deserved short break by the sea. The tide was well out when she took her early morning dip. As she splashed her way back through the shallows she saw a distant figure jogging along the shore. As the track suited figure came closer Sindy saw that the jogger was a girl. By the time she reached the water's edge, the girl was close enough for Sindy to recognise her.

"Mandy!" she exclaimed.

"Sindy!" panted the girl, equally surprised. "I didn't expect to see you here!"

"Likewise!" Sindy replied. "I thought you were still in hospital!"

"M-made a remarkable recovery," panted Mandy, jogging on the spot.

Sindy thought she looked ready to drop. She offered her a cup of coffee. "There's some in the pot!" she said. "My caravan is just over that dune!"

Mandy declined the offer. She said that she had better keep going. The quicker she got fitter, the sooner she would be back in the saddle.

"Don't you think that you might be over doing things a bit?" remarked Sindy.

"Another week and I'll be as fit as you, Sindy!" panted Mandy. "I'm glad I've met up with someone I know. I was beginning to get lonely here on my own!"

"Tell you what, Mandy," said Sindy, wishing that her friend would stop jogging, "if you won't stop for coffee why not join me in a picnic? I know a lovely little cove along the coast. I'll pick you up in the Range Rover about tennish by the marina."

"Super!" puffed Mandy, as she started to jog off again. "See you later, Sindy!"

Sindy picked up her beach wrap and looked towards the jogging figure. "I don't think that I'd be in such a hurry to get back into show jumping if what happened to Mandy happened to me!" she thought.

Mandy Maltravers was one of the top horsewomen in show jumping, but even the best riders have accidents. It was not so much the fall that had caused her serious injuries, it was the behaviour of her horse after it had thrown her. It had suddenly gone berserk, charging round the arena, lashing out at everything with its flying hooves, including Mandy. Firebrand, the big piebald stallion, certainly lived up to his reputation that evening. Mandy was not the first rider the big tempestuous beast had put in hospital. Why had Mandy been so keen to buy him when he was put up for sale? She knew a good jumper when she saw one, as did his previous owner, which was why Mandy could only afford to put up part of the money to buy him. Others had been quite willing to put the rest. Mandy and Firebrand seemed like a good investment. On good days the big horse was practically unbeatable. There were one or two big events coming up, which was why Mandy was pushing herself to get fit. She knew the co-owners had their eyes on the big prize money. She also knew that they would be just as anxious to get rid of him to recoup their money, as they were to jump on the bandwaggon, should he misbehave again.

"I'm sure that you are pushing yourself too hard, Mandy," said Sindy over their picnic lunch.

"Nonsense!" retorted Mandy. "I'm fit enough to beat you at any sport you care to choose!"

"I've got a better idea," smiled Sindy. "Lets you and I just sunbathe and see who tans the quickest!"

So for the rest of the afternoon that's just what they did. Although Mandy would not admit it, Sindy knew that she was feeling all the better for relaxing.

When Sindy suggested that they might go to a disco that evening, Mandy told her that she had already made plans. There was show jumping on the t.v. and she invited Sindy to watch it with her in the hotel lounge. Sindy politely declined. Keen horsewoman though she was, she preferred to go to the disco on her own, than spend her evening sat in front of a television in a stuffy hotel lounge. Anyway, if she wanted to watch t.v. she could do so in her own caravan.

It was a warm summer's evening. Far too nice to spend in a hotel lounge. In fact, Sindy decided it was even too nice to waste it at a disco. She would go for another swim, after which she would cook herself some supper, and maybe take a stroll along the shore.

She had had her swim and was wading ashore when she saw, as she had that morning, a figure hurrying along the beach. It was Mandy. This time she was not wearing a track suit, nor was she jogging. She was running. She could hardly catch her breath when she spoke to Sindy. She had been out numbered by the other hotel guests as to what programme they were going to watch. So could she watch the show jumping on Sindy's t.v.?

"Be my guest!" Sindy replied. "I'll be right with you when I've had a quick shower, and fixed us both some supper! You must be crazy to run all that way!"

"I didn't want to miss it," gasped Mandy.

Sindy switched on the set and left Mandy to watch it. She had just stepped under the shower when Mandy called to her to come quickly. Sindy grabbed a towel, and wondered what on earth could be the matter. She arrived in time to see Firebrand canter into the arena with a young man in the saddle. Mandy could hardly contain herself.

"The idiots!" she screamed. "Why couldn't they wait? If Firebrand takes it into his head to play up he won't know what to do!"

Sindy recognised the rider. It was Mostyn Smith. Sindy knew him quite well.

"Calm down, Mandy," she said. "Mostyn has been around a long time! You are getting het up over nothing!"

It appeared that Sindy was right. The big horse jumped two clear rounds with no effort at all. Wrapped in her towel, Sindy forgot her shower, as she sat down to watch the jump-off against the clock. Firebrand was the first to go.

"Gosh! Look at him go!" gasped Sindy. "At that speed he's unbeatable!"

With only the wall to jump it appeared to be all over, then as Mostyn Smith pulled him round, the big horse suddenly reared. Mostyn managed to stay on but not for long. He would have suffered the same fate as Mandy but for the swift action of some of the arena party.

"I knew it! I knew it!" screamed Mandy.

"Take it easy!" said Sindy.

"Don't just stand there telling me what to do," shouted Mandy. "Hurry up and get dressed. We've got to get up to London!"

"Whatever for?" Sindy asked puzzled.

Mandy glowered back at her. "Don't stand there asking stupid questions! Are you coming or aren't you?"

Then muttering that she could not wait for Sindy to make up her mind she jumped down out of the caravan leaving Sindy standing, open mouthed.

"Hang on a minute!" she cried. "I can't go up to London like this!"

Sindy heard the door of her Range Rover slam. She darted for the door. The engine started. Clutching the towel to her, Sindy ran towards the vehicle. Too late. Mandy was away, full tilt across the field towards the road. Without the Range Rover Sindy was stranded. She stood wondering what she should do. Should she go to the police? If she called in the police it was sure to land Mandy in trouble. Mandy was a good friend.

"She hasn't exactly stolen my Range Rover," she said to herself. "Anyway, I've only got myself to blame. I shouldn't have left the keys in it. I can only hope that she doesn't have an accident, and trust that she brings it back!"

Sindy thought for a moment and then decided what she would do. If she had to go to the police she would put it off until the morning. She finished her shower, dressed and then settled down to supper.

It was in the early hours of the morning that Mandy returned with the Range Rover. It was a very repentant Mandy who roused Sindy. Could she ever forgive her? Sindy was relieved to know that she was all right. She told Sindy that she had every right to call the police.

"I thought about it," Sindy smiled. "But please don't give me any more shocks!"

"I am afraid you might be in for another," Mandy replied, pointing towards the Range Rover. Sindy suddenly realised there was a horse box hitched to her vehicle.

"I've brought Firebrand back with me," Mandy said.

"What?" gasped Sindy. "You haven't stolen him have you?"

"No! He's now all mine! I got him for a song, although I'm afraid he has cost me just about everything I own!"

"You must be out of your mind," Sindy exclaimed. "His show jumping days are over. You heard them say so on the telly!"

"That's what the others said too. They were all set to sell him to a wealthy American breeder. I only got there in time to stop the deal going through," Mandy replied. "We'll have him jumping again, Sindy. You'll see!"

"We?" enquired Sindy.

It appeared that Mandy had got it all worked out. If Sindy was agreeable, Firebrand would be stabled at her manor house, and as part repayment she would be Sindy's housekeeper when Sindy was away on business. Once she and the horse were on their feet she would repay Sindy back in full.

"What happens if I don't agree?" asked Sindy.

"Firebrand will be shipped to America, or put down, and I will have made myself penniless for nothing," Mandy replied.

"A friend in need is a friend indeed," quoted Sindy with a grin. "Of course I agree, but on one condition!"

"What's that?" asked Mandy.

"You stop trying to do too much," Sindy replied. "You can stay on at the manor house as long as you want!"

Firebrand seemed to settle down quite happily at Sindy's manor house. Sindy soon had him eating out of her hand. It was hard to believe that he was the terror he could sometimes be. The fine spell of weather continued on a bit longer, before it started to become sultry.

It was the quiet before the storm the afternoon Mandy decided to saddle up Firebrand and ride him. The storm clouds were building up as she took him over the jumps in the paddock. There was a faint rumble of thunder in the distance.

"You'd better call it a day!" called Sindy. "You're going to get drenched shortly!"

"One more round," laughed Mandy.

"We'll see if we can beat the rain drops!"

There was a brilliant flash of lightning. The big horse reared, and Mandy was thrown. Sindy watched horrified as the big animal leapt the paddock rails, jumped the hedge at the end of the field and charged off into the wood beyond, just as the heavens opened up. Her first thoughts were for her friend. Mandy's were for the horse.

"I'm all right, Sindy!" she cried. "Go after him!"

Sindy put her friend first before the horse. Both were drenched when they got to the house.

"Please, Sindy," said Mandy, "go and look for Firebrand for me!"

Sindy was already drenched to her skin so she did not bother to put a raincoat on. By the time she reached the wood the storm had abated a little. She expected to hear the big horse crashing through the undergrowth. She followed his trail of destruction until she saw him standing still. He turned his head and saw her. He started to paw the ground.

"This is it!" thought Sindy. "He's going to take it out on me!"

She shot behind the nearest tree and waited. Firebrand did not charge. He limped quietly in her direction, and nuzzled her.

Mandy was hobbling, too, when Sindy brought the big horse back. Unconcerned about her own injury, she thought only of the horse. They would have to call in a vet. It might be a costly business. Sindy told Mandy of an old groom she knew in the village. He often saw to her horses. She would fetch him so that he could take a look, then if they needed they'd call in a vet.

Within the hour, old Jack, the groom, strolled up to Firebrand.

"Hello, old son!" he said. "Remember me? If you don't I expect your old mum does if she's still alive and kickin'! Right, let's see what you've been an' gone an' done!"

"You mean you know him, Jack?" asked a surprised Sindy.

"I ought to, Miss Sindy!" old Jack replied. "I helped bring him into the world!"

Old Jack then examined the now docile horse. His verdict was a bruised fetlock. "Nowt to bother a vet about," he chuckled. "I'll have 'im as right as rain again in a few days!"

Old Jack's fee? A strong mug of tea. As he sat drinking it, he and the girls chatted.

"Have you any idea why he plays up like he does?" asked Mandy.

"Lightnin', miss! He don't like lightnin'! Him an' his mum were nearly struck by it when 'im was young! It were one 'ell of a storm! I thought we were all done for!"

That certainly explained his behaviour that afternoon, but there had never been a storm when he had gone berserk in the show rings. So why had he?

It was a few days later during a fashion show that the answer came to Sindy. Flash bulbs were popping as the models were displaying the clothes. Photographs were always being taken at ring side and the glare from the flashes must be responsible for frightening Firebrand.

Back from the fashion show Sindy put her theory to the test. The big horse did not bat an eyelid. It could not be that. Sindy was not so sure.

Through her t.v. connections she got hold of videos of some of the show jumping programmes. Played through slowly, she and Mandy watched for the flashes. After playing them over and over again to make sure, they were positive that on each occasion one flash was more brilliant than most. Next they traced the photographer, a young man, who always sat in the front row of the arena. Mandy thought Sindy was crazy when she said that she would track the young man down. She was sure that he was responsible, and doing it deliberately. Why should he? That was what Sindy intended to find out.

Sindy knew a lot of photographers. While Mandy stayed to train Firebrand, Sindy stayed up in town, and at every opportunity showed her photographer friends a blow up of the young man with the camera. It seemed an impossible task, but Sindy stuck to it.

One evening a young man called at her flat. It was the young man she had been looking for. He mistakingly thought Sindy had been asking after him because she wanted him for a job. He had brought along an album filled with his samples.

"You certainly have picked the right man," he said, as he watched Sindy thumb through the photographs.

"I certainly have!" Sindy replied, spotting a picture of Firebrand throwing a rider headlong into a jump. "I would like you to come with me to my manor house in the country, and bring these with you! I have a friend who would be very interested to see these!"

Thinking he was onto an assignment the young man readily agreed.

He got more than he bargained for when he met Mandy.

"I've got a living to make!" he squealed, when she confronted him.

"And you don't care who nearly gets killed so long as you are making money," Mandy snapped back. "I've a mind to put you on that horse's back and use your flash, and see how you fare! Now you clear out of here . . . No, I'm keeping these pictures. Try anything like that again and you're finished!"

How did the young man know about Firebrand's reactions to lightning? They found out from old Jack the following day. He'd seen the young man hurrying to the station.

"He used to live at the stables where Firebrand were reared. He know'd about 'is fear o' lightnin'. I mind the time 'is old dad gave 'im a thick ear for annoyin' the 'orses!" he said, sipping his tea.

It was time for Firebrand to earn his keep. He was ready to enter the show jumping events again. However, there just one problem. Mandy was not quite fit enough yet to ride him.

It looked like being an ideal day at the open air show jumping ground at Wickstead, but when the jumping event Sindy and Firebrand were entered for started, storm clouds were looming on the horizon.

"Don't worry about a thing," Mandy told her before she entered the ring. "Just enjoy yourself out there! I'll watch out for that horrid photographer. It'll be him not you who'll be going to hospital if I see him! I wish I was up there in the saddle instead of you!"

"Likewise!" said Sindy, eyeing the storm clouds.

The starting bell rang, and the big horse was off. He cleared the jumps without any trouble. Firebrand was the best jumper that she'd ever ridden. She was rather looking forward to the next round.

"You'll get no trouble from your photographer friend," Mandy told her. "I've just had him thrown out of the ground!"

Sindy was sure she heard thunder as they were jumping the second round. Firebrand had pricked his ears, she thought, but it didn't put him off his stride. Another clear round.

Sindy watched the big bank of cloud as they altered the course for the jump-off against the clock. Her heart sank when she found out that they were the last to go. Thunder was definitely rumbling when they entered the ring, with an almost impossible time to beat. Just as the bell rang, lightning forked in the sky. Firebrand was away like a rocket. Sindy could hear the crowd shouting. Suddenly she realised the horse was not bolting. Firebrand was jumping the course. A loud clap of thunder. The storm was getting nearer. Sindy decided to get it over with as quick as she could. Faults or not, the sooner they were out of the arena the better.

"Go, Firebrand! Go," she shouted.

The big horse certainly went. Any other horse would have ploughed through the course. Not Firebrand. He cleared all the obstacles as if they were not there. They were still cheering when they left the arena.

"What were you trying to do, break the sound barrier!" laughed Mandy. "I'm glad you are not competing all the time. I'd have a job keeping up with you!" Mandy handed all the prize money over to Sindy, who firmly handed it back.

"I'll just hang onto the rosette, so that I can say Firebrand stayed at my stable when you and he become famous!"

Sindy Fashion Feature – the Emanuels

David and Elizabeth Emanuel rose to fame when they were chosen by the Princess of Wales to design her wedding dress. Since then, famous people from around the world have descended on their salon to have original and unique dresses designed and made for them.

It was obvious, therefore, that when I wanted some new clothes for myself that it was to the Emanuels I should go. After having the dresses designed I then went back to talk to them about their work, their ideas and how they got started.

Sindy: I must say it was exciting having a collection of dresses especially designed for me. Tell me something about them.

Elizabeth: Well, we knew that you like to go to lots of parties and so we called the first of our ball gowns for you, *'High Society'*. It's a fuschia pink with matching cape both trimmed with a deep frill and pink bows. And we gave you a matching pair of pink high heeled shoes to go with it, as well as a single strand diamante necklace. *'Misty Mauve'* was more dramatic. In lilac, it has a three tiered skirt with a lilac net underskirt and a sweetheart shaped bodice in black velvet trimmed with a lilac rosebud. There's also a black velvet cloak lined in matching lilac material.

Sindy: It was terribly exciting coming to the salon for the fitting. Tell me about the other two dresses, David.

David: *'Scarlet Lady'* is the kind of dress that'll really make people notice you. It's in scarlet with a black velvet bodice trimmed with a red neck frill and bow. And the black velvet cloak is lined in the same material.

'Romantica' is in honey silk and has what we call a scoop neckline, two tiered skirt and shoulder wrap. We also gave you a single strand diamante necklace to wear with it, which sets if off perfectly.

Sindy: What really fascinated

Four dresses designed for me by the Emanuels. Here 'High Society'.

me is the trouble you go to in getting everything right when someone like myself comes to the salon. What is the full proceedure?
Elizabeth: We hate to rush things, although it is possible for us to make something quickly if required, provided, of course, it is a fairly simple design. But the one-offs that we do usually take much longer and a lot of care goes into making certain that everything is right.

So the first step when someone comes to see us is to sit down and discuss exactly what the dress is for. It might be for a special party or a film presentation or whatever.
Sindy: Do you make sketches there and then?
David: We work on some rough ideas with the client and we go a step further by showing them video films of shows of our collections that we've already done. This gives them an idea of what they might be looking for, although it won't be a copy of anything they see.
Sindy: So once I've decided what style of dress I want, what then?
Elizabeth: Then we'd discuss specific things about the dress, such as whether you would like a scoop neckline or a 'V' neck or bouffant.
Sindy: I suppose the fabrics are the next stage. That was marvellous for me, I never realised there were so many beautiful materials to choose from.
David: We keep quite a few materials in stock which might well turn out to be just the thing you were looking for. Or you might want something similar but in a different colour, in which case we have to arrange for the material.
Sindy: Do you travel around the world much looking for new fabrics?
Elizabeth: Quite a lot. We go to Italy quite frequently and once a year we go to Japan because we have a ready-to-wear arrangement there which we have discussions about. But, yes, we are always on the look out for new materials.
Sindy: So I now know what I roughly want and what I'd like it in. Then I'm measured, is that right?
David: That's correct. And then we make what we call a toile. This is a mock-up of the dress in a kind of calico material. Not the real thing, but exact in most details.
Sindy: Why do you do this and not just make the dress?
Elizabeth: Because it gives you and us the opportunity to change anything before we do the real thing. You can alter the whole thing at this stage. Once we've agreed on the final touches we then go ahead and make the dress and you'd come back for a couple of fittings. From start to finish it would probably have taken a couple of months.
Sindy: Do you ever do the cutting yourself?
David: We're trained to do everything. But we don't do so much cutting of the materials ourselves now. Although recently one of our cutters had to leave and I was sitting up for all hours of the night doing it myself.
Sindy: I know that you do one-off dresses which you refuse to copy for anyone else. Has anyone tried to ask you to

'Romantica' — note the single strand diamante necklace I wear with this dress.

'Misty Mauve'— a feature of this outfit is the sweetheart shaped bodice in black velvet.

do a copy?
Elizabeth: When we did a black off-the-shoulder dress for the Princess of Wales we had requests from around the world, but we refused to copy it!
Sindy: What was one of the most difficult dresses you did other than the wedding dress for the Princess of Wales?
David: It was another wedding dress, but for an Arab Lady. Real jewels had to be sewn into it. In other instances we have had to employ a team of people to sew hundreds of beads onto a bodice.
Sindy: Where do you get your ideas from. You like delving back into history, don't you?
Elizabeth: We've always loved going to museums and looking at the costumes. We also read a lot of books on the subject and are influenced by things we see when we're abroad.
Sindy: Does the personality of the person who wants a dress from you influence how you make it for them?
David: I don't think you can avoid it. A person must feel at home with a dress and therefore it must suit her personality.
Sindy: So tell me, David, how did you get into dress designing?
David: Through art school. I was born in Glamorgan into quite a large family. I've ten brothers and a sister. I did a lot of singing, being Welsh, and travelled around the country performing at festivals.
Sindy: Did you win any prizes?
David: Yes, quite a few. I also played piano and violin. But I was really set on going to the Royal College of Art. To do that I went to Harrow School of Art first, which is where I met Elizabeth.
Sindy: Was art your first love, too?
Elizabeth: It was. But I also enjoyed horse riding and ballet. I studied with the Ballet Rambert and learnt to ride when I was quite young.
Sindy: Did you go in for showjumping competitions?
Elizabeth: Lots of them. I won prizes at the Royal International and the Horse of the Year Show. But it was art that I wanted to do most for a career.
Sindy: So you met at the same art school?
David: Yes. Then we got married and knew that some day we'd love to own our own salon.
Sindy: Well you've certainly realised all of your ambitions. Was the first day of opening your salon exciting?
Elizabeth: Oh, yes. And hectic. We were in such a rush to show off our new collection to some important people that the carpet was still being laid on the salon floor just an hour before they arrived. We made it in time, though!
Sindy: Some people look on your dresses as they would a painting, and collect them like that, is that true?
David: I don't know about that. It's flattering if they do. But three of our dresses are exhibited at the Metropolitan Museum in New York, the Victoria and Albert Museum in London, and the Royal Ontario Museum in Canada.
Sindy: You can be certain I'll always keep mine.

'Scarlet Lady'— a striking dress that is guaranteed to get me noticed.

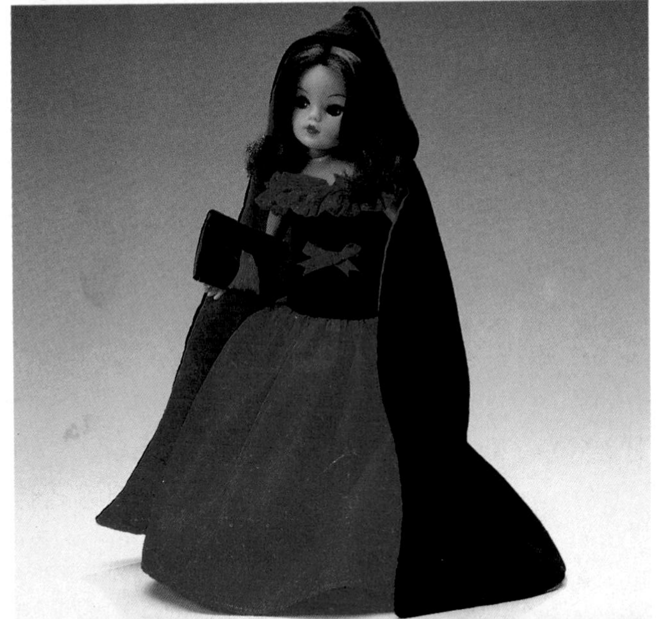

Sindy's Happy Hair Care

I don't want to sound big-headed, but people often tell me how fantastic my hair looks, and I like to think that it's because I take good care of it.

Not many of us are really happy with our hair — it's either too dry or too greasy, the wrong colour or too straight or curly. I must say, long hair like mine does take a lot of looking after, and even though I'm lucky that I can do so many different styles with it, I've been tempted several times to have it snipped off when I've seen a short style that I really love!

Sometimes Mum can seem to be your biggest enemy when it comes to your hair, but a friend of mine taught me that if I was clever, my Mum could be my best friend in that respect! Well, honestly, Mums never like us to look way-out, but they love to give us advice and never mind how we have our hair as long as it suits us — and I agree! Well, I'd look pretty silly with a black spiky style, wouldn't I? So, my first tip is talk to your Mum (and your hairdresser) and get her on your side and . . . *listen*!

Getting a good cut is the first step — and this is really where you should leave it up to your hairdresser. Cut some different styles from pictures in magazines, so that you have a choice, but be sensible about it and agree to have the cut which will suit you best. After that, go along to the salon every two months regularly to keep it in good shape. *Everyone* gets split ends and we're all better off without them!

Step two is shampooing. Now, that may sound easy (not to mention boring!), but I didn't realise how important such a simple thing is. You *must* use the right shampoo for your hair type. Ask your hairdresser if you're not sure, but Mum will be able to tell you too. If you've got 'dry' hair use a special moisturising dry-hair shampoo — the same goes if it's 'greasy'. If you really have 'normal' hair (lucky you!) don't go looking for anything special — you don't need it. Some people like to wash their hair every day for freshness or to give it body, so if you're one of them, choose a shampoo marked 'mild'. There are so many different shampoos in the shops now, that you'll be better off asking Mum to help you find one that's right for you and good value too! By the way, all of us get dandruff from time to time, so for goodness sake keep a medicated shampoo at home for emergencies and *use* it! But the most important way to stop dandruff is eat a healthy diet and wash your brushes and combs every time you wash your hair. Whatever you do, don't use too much of *any* shampoo. A 10p-sized blob is enough, and two light shampoos are better than one.

Next, don't forget conditioner! It might seem expensive to use this on top of the right shampoo, but it's worth it. Make sure you rinse your hair well after washing it, and then pour out another 10p-sized blob of conditioner and massage it well into your scalp. A good tip is to comb it through when you've rubbed it all in, and then count to sixty. Always use the matching conditioner to your shampoo. You may be thinking that you've got a problem at this stage. Perhaps Mum only buys one sort of shampoo for the whole family? Maybe she doesn't buy any conditioner? Have a talk to her and tell her that you like to keep your hair healthy and looking nice, and if she *can't* help then say that you would like some special shampoos and conditioners for your birthday and at Christmas. The other way is to save up your pocket money and cut out sweets! Then hide your bottles away!

If you have difficult hair which never seems to do what you want it to, then use some gel or mousse when you're styling it. They help to settle hair down and give it more body. You only need to use these occasionally to help you manage. Try to let your hair dry naturally — blow drying it too much can damage it.

Finally, three old fashioned tips for you! If you have greasy hair, squeeze fresh lemon juice into your last rinse, especially if you're blonde, or use vinegar if you have dark or normal hair . . . but to get the best shine of all, rinse off with *cold* water! It works . . . *honestly*!

Sindy Meets Wham!

It was just eight in the morning when my editor rang me. "Sindy," he said. "We need a special pop feature for the Annual and Wham! have agreed to an interview providing you can get to Heathrow Airport before eleven. They're off on a world tour and won't be back in the country for weeks." Wham! The chance to meet those two gorgeous guys, George and Andrew. I was up, showered, dressed and on my way to Heathrow within the hour. On arrival I was ushered into the V.I.P. lounge where George and Andrew were waiting. They greeted me with a friendly 'Hi' and within seconds we were chatting away like old friends.

Sindy: Do you ever get tired of being bothered by your fans, Andy?
Andy: I think that the time to start being bothered is when they don't come up and want autographs or to chat to you. I mean, if you go into pop music you must know that the people who buy your records build up a kind of friendship with you, even if you've never met. So it's only natural that the fans'll do all they can to make certain they do see you.
Sindy: But can you ever have any time to yourself?
Andy: Oh, yes. What does get a bit tiring is when I go home and find that my parents have invited some fans indoors for a cup of tea to wait for me. There I am thinking that I've managed to find a few moments to myself and suddenly I'm back in the throng again. My parents find it difficult to appreciate how many people need a slice of your time. They're on the side of the fans. It's funny, really, they don't like to see them disappointed.
Sindy: You haven't gone out and bought yourself a huge house then, George?
George: Not until recently. I was quite happy living at home. But both Andy and I live a distance from London where most of our business is conducted. So we contemplated buying a flat nearer in order to be just a short ride from the centre of things. Now, though, I've been looking for a house nearer my home town and it'll be fun having it all decorated and choosing furniture.
Sindy: Are either of you considering leaving the country to live abroad?
Andy: We love England, but George does like America, particularly New York and he keeps on saying how much he'd love to live there for at least part of the time. Whether he will, however, is another thing!
Sindy: You certainly had a huge hit with *'Careless Whisper'* in America, George. How did you feel about that?
George: It was marvellous! We'd tried to break into the American record charts before but didn't have too much success. That was soon after we recorded *'Young Guns'*. The record made a slight impression and we did a number of television shows

there. But *'Careless Whisper'* suddenly shot up the charts and really made a marvellous prize for us after four consecutive hits in Britain.
Sindy: That song was a solo by you, George. Did a lot of people think that *'Wham!'* would be breaking up?
George: Some did. But there's absolutely no truth in the rumour at all. Andy and I consider that whatever we do as individuals on record, it is still a *'Wham!'* thing.
Sindy: Did it worry you, Andy?
Andy: Not at all. George has got a better voice than I have and the song was more suited to his style than to a *'Wham!'* one.
Sindy: You seem to like taking lots of holidays?
George: What we do is this. When we have to go abroad to work, whether it's touring or making a video film, we always try and make certain that we add a few days to relax. That way we see a bit of the places we visit instead of just being stuck in studios or hotel rooms and we can keep ourselves fit and fresh too!
Sindy: Don't the fans notice you when you're on holiday?
George: Sometimes. I remember that when we had to go to Spain to work for a couple of weeks, Andy managed to accidentally tell millions of television watchers of a programme just when and where we were going. When we got there we found thousands of people following us around. It was quite a laugh really. And when I went to Cyprus for a holiday I didn't think anyone would know me, but they receive all the music papers there and I spent half my time doing interviews!
Sindy: Do the pair of you ever argue much, Andy?
Andy: No. We might have the occasional disagreement, but we've been together since schooldays and know each other so well that we understand each other perfectly well. Any time we do find ourselves going that way we usually end up laughing.
Sindy: What did you think of Andy when you first met him, George?
George: I saw him at school and thought that he was someone I'd really like to get to know. Soon we found we had similar tastes in most things, and mostly music and we were always together, going to dances and things like that!
Sindy: You both seem to be very honest about your work as pop stars.
George: Why not? We don't pretend to be anything. We see ourselves as entertainers and when we put on a stage show we act the part of being pop stars. The problem is that some people believe we're like that all of the time.
Sindy: When you do concerts you usually put on a film show of yourselves. Why?
Andy: It's all a bit of a laugh. We are always making home movies. We thought it'd be a bit of fun for the fans to see us when we were younger and the kind of things we got up to. We still make movies of ourselves around the world.

Word Search

T	H	N	I	G	H	T	D	R	E	S	S	E	H	A	N	D	B	A	G
T	W	E	N	T	Y	R	E	I	G	H	T	I	T	E	M	S	O	F	S
S	I	N	D	B	L	O	U	S	E	Y	S	J	O	D	H	P	U	R	S
C	S	L	O	T	H	U	I	N	G	Y	S	O	U	R	A	R	E	L	O
O	U	N	D	E	R	S	L	I	P	K	K	I	N	E	G	R	F	O	R
A	N	R	E	B	U	E	T	A	F	M	I	N	I	S	K	I	R	T	E
W	T	T	O	B	E	R	F	H	O	U	P	N	D	S	I	D	N	T	S
H	O	E	C	F	A	S	B	A	U	L	A	O	U	E	S	I	S	I	O
N	P	L	A	Y	S	U	I	T	D	Y	N	C	O	S	L	N	L	E	C
C	T	I	S	O	N	I	T	H	E	R	T	E	A	R	A	G	A	L	K
T	U	T	U	S	O	T	R	A	C	K	S	U	I	T	A	J	W	H	S
O	L	E	A	R	A	N	G	E	O	F	F	A	S	J	E	A	N	S	H
I	B	O	L	E	R	O	O	N	A	S	N	D	S	C	E	C	N	W	E
S	E	T	C	T	I	N	G	A	C	C	C	S	E	S	S	K	O	I	R
I	E	C	L	O	A	K	S	B	E	A	C	H	R	O	B	E	P	M	L
U	S	T	O	W	O	F	A	B	U	R	L	O	O	U	S	T	H	S	O
L	E	O	T	A	R	D	U	S	E	F	S	E	A	H	N	D	A	U	W
H	O	L	H	E	R	A	N	G	B	E	O	S	F	A	F	U	R	I	N
I	E	V	E	N	I	N	G	G	O	W	N	T	U	T	I	G	H	T	S
R	E	F	S	O	R	Y	O	U	A	T	O	P	L	A	Y	W	I	T	H

Can you find the following 28 items of clothing from Sindy's wardrobe in the grid above?
Answers on page 63.

Nightdress
Handbag
Blouse
Jodhpurs
Underslip
Miniskirt
Scarf

Playsuit
Tutu
Tracksuit
Jeans
Bolero
Cloak
Boa

Beachrobe
Leotard
Evening Gown
Tights
Trouser Suit
Dresses
Hat

Sun-top
Ski-pants
Riding Jacket
Casual clothes
Socks
Swimsuit
Shoes

Sindy's Giddy Aunt

Sindy was returning after putting her two horses in the paddock at the rear of her manor house when a big white Rolls Royce glided into the drive. "Whoever is it?" she said to Rufus, her red setter dog. "I'm not expecting anyone!"

Rufus started to bark. Sindy had a job to hold him back. A uniformed chauffeur was gingerly getting out of the car.

"Er-is that dog dangerous, miss?" he nervously asked.

"That depends on the caller and what their business is!" Sindy replied.

"My goodness! It's Sindy," exclaimed a female voice from inside the car.

The chauffeur hurriedly opened the door and out stepped a well groomed woman. "Sindy!" she exclaimed again. "You of all people! What a lovely surprise!"

Sindy was almost overcome by her expensive perfume when the woman embraced her.

"Somebody said that you had buried yourself in the country. When I told Bates to stop at the first house we came to I never expected to meet a dear friend!"

Sindy stood bewildered. She could not recall ever seeing her well groomed, highly perfumed visitor before, yet by the greeting she had just received, she felt that she must have done. Sindy had many friends. She was usually quick to recognise them but not this one. Who could she possibly be?

Sindy hoped that she would say something that would give her a clue. Although she appeared to have a lot to say, there was no mention of anything that revealed her identity. Was she an actress, or was she someone well up in the fashion world?

"She must be," thought Sindy, "to use that sort of perfume, and wear earrings like those!"

Like big crystal tear drops they were. Sindy was sure she had seen those earrings somewhere before. Maybe if she mentioned them, the woman might say something that would reveal who she was.

"Yes, they are rather unique!" was all she said before hurriedly changing the subject to the reason for the surprise visit.

"You know how scatter-brained I can be, Sindy!" she began. "It was only after passing through the last village that it suddenly dawned on me that I had not telephoned my friend up in London that I was coming. We stopped at the public call box at the end of your lane only to find that the silly contraption was out of order. It was then I had a brainwave. I told Bates to stop at the next habitation which looked as if it might have a telephone. Imagine my surprise and delight when it turned out to be yours. Would you mind awfully if I gave my friend a tinkle?"

"Er-not at all," replied Sindy, still trying to think who her visitor might be. "If you care to follow me! Be careful on the steps!"

The woman followed Sindy up the steps to the living accommodation on the upper floor.

"What a charming place, Sindy! I do admire your taste!"

Sindy thanked her for the compliment and directed her to the telephone in the living room, before retiring to the kitchen. Curious though she was, Sindy had no wish to eaves drop on the telephone conversation. Even so she heard just about everything the woman said but nothing that gave her a clue as to her identity. The conversation over, she joined Sindy in her super kitchen.

"Mm! I smell coffee in the pot," she said. "I'm just dying for a cup!"

"Sorry," replied Sindy. "Whatever could I have been thinking of not to have offered you one!"

"Have you something on your mind?" asked the visitor.

Indeed Sindy had, but she was not letting on as to what it was. It was the earrings. Sindy was now more than sure that she had seen them many times before.

"What a splendid home you have," remarked her visitor, as Sindy handed her the coffee. "Somebody said that you had done a fantastic job with the decor. Mind if I do a quick tour?"

Whether Sindy minded or not, her visitor was off, peeking in every room, and full of admiration for everything she saw. "When next you are up in London, you must pop round to my town house and give me a few tips, Sindy dear!"

Sindy could not contain her curiosity any longer.

"I hope you won't think me stupid or rude, or that you won't mind me asking . . ."

Sindy's visitor cut her short. Thrusting the empty coffee cup in her hand, she said she had to dash. No embrace this time. Just a quick peck on Sindy's cheek and she was heading for the door. By the time Sindy reached the top of the steps her well groomed visitor was nearly to the car. Such was her haste that she stumbled and nearly fell. The chauffeur appeared to be about to bundle her into the back of the Rolls Royce when he realised that Sindy was watching. Quickly they both gathered their composure. She gave Sindy a wave and thanked her for her hospitality as the chauffeur ushered her in before hurrying round to the driving seat. Sindy took note of the car's registration number plate as it pulled out of the drive. Sindy was suspicious. She was in two minds to inform the police.

She might have done if she had not been side-tracked. Hardly had the car departed when she heard her telephone ringing. It was Sindy's friend Glenda. She had got herself a problem. She had taken her car to the garage for a minor repair and had been promised it would be ready when she called for it that morning. Glenda had just been to the garage only to be told that it now wouldn't be ready till the evening. So what was the problem?

Glenda was taking flying lessons and was due for one that afternoon, but she had no means of getting out to the airfield. Could Sindy help her out?

"Okay, Glenda! I'll be happy to oblige!" said Sindy. "About what time?"

Sindy was told that if she came at once Glenda would treat her to lunch out at the flying club.

"In that case I'll be on my way as soon as I've washed up the coffee cups and locked the house up!"

"Coffee cups, Sindy? Have you been entertaining?"

Sindy mentioned her mysterious visitor and promised to tell Glenda everything over lunch.

Sindy found the big tear drop earring in the drive when she went to the garage. What should she do? Should she wait in case its owner returned? She might have to wait for ages. If the woman was as scatter-brained as she made herself out to be she might not even realise she had mislaid it. Sindy decided to take the earring with her for safe keeping, and leave Rufus at home. If her visitor did turn up she would just have to wait until Sindy got back.

As Sindy approached the road junction at the end of the lane she saw Mrs. Martin from one of the cottages opposite, stepping out of the call box. Mrs. Martin recognised Sindy's Range Rover and waved. Sindy stopped and offered her a lift into the village.

"I can drop you off at the post office. You can make your call from there!"

"Whatever for, dearie?" the good lady asked, somewhat surprised. "I've only just rung up my sister from here!"

Once again Sindy's suspicions were roused.

On the way to the flying club, and over lunch, Sindy told her friend Glenda about her mysterious visitor, of her suspicions, and her intention to inform the police.

"If I had as many friends as you have, Sindy, I'd have a job remembering who they all were!" Glenda said. "By your description of her I'd say she is high up in the fashion world and she was wearing the earrings when you were introduced to each other at some junket or other!"

"You might be right," Sindy replied, "but I still think I ought to inform the police."

"If it puts your mind at ease go ahead, but a thief would find it easier to break into Fort Knox than your home. I've often wondered how you yourself would get in if ever you locked yourself out. If you want the 'phone it's in the foyer."

The 'phone was already in use when Sindy went into the foyer. She hoped the caller would not be long. A voice behind her advised

her that it would be quicker if she went home and used her own phone. "When Mavis gets talking to her boyfriend they can bill and coo the whole afternoon. What brings you out to the flying club, Sindy? Thinking of taking up flying? In case you are wondering who I am, I'm Dave Travis. We met at one of Glenda's parties!"

Sindy remembered the friendly young man. How could she forget? He was the one who accidentally spilled coke down her dress. When she told him that she had brought Glenda out for her flying lesson, he offered to make amends.

"Like to come up with me in my micro light? It will be more fun than waiting for Mavis to come off that 'phone, or hanging around until Glenda comes down!"

"Why not?" thought Sindy, and she agreed. She had never flown in a micro light before. It would be a new experience.

"My giddy aunt!" exclaimed Glenda, when Sindy told her. "You must be out of your tiny mind, Sindy! You wouldn't get me up in the air

in that contraption!"

It was then that Glenda's instructor appeared. He put Sindy's mind at ease. "You'll be as safe as houses with young Travis, miss! Have a good trip!"

As Sindy stood on her own the expression Glenda used kept running through her mind. "My giddy aunt!" As she thrust her hand in her pocket and felt the earring, her memory suddenly clicked. My giddy aunt was the expression she used to describe her zany Aunt Lucy. Aunt Lucy wore big tear drop earrings. Sindy was always fascinated by them. They had cost Uncle Owen a small fortune, but he reckoned they were worth every penny if they slowed Aunt Lucy down. It was never Aunt Lucy who had called on her that morning, yet she felt almost sure that the earring in her hand was one of the same pair. How did the mystery woman happen to be wearing them?

Dave Travis disturbed her thoughts. As soon as Sindy was ready, they'd be off. The little aircraft had hardly moved before Sindy realised that they were airborne.

"How would you like to fly over your house, Sindy?" the young pilot shouted.

Sindy could hardly hear him above the drone of the tiny engine.

"Yes please!" Sindy yelled back. "It's about two miles on the other side of the village!"

Sindy found micro light flying quite exhilarating. It was funny to look down and see the people below looking up to see what it was that was buzzing over.

"See anything you recognise, Sindy?" shouted Travis. "Are we headed in the right direction?"

Sindy spotted the big wood with the lake where sometimes she walked Rufus, or rode her horses. If Travis carried straight on they would fly right over the manor house.

He gave Sindy the thumbs up sign and a great big grin. Sindy looked down as they approached the lake. Parked close to it was a big white car. A couple were sunbathing on the grass close by. Sindy wondered if they knew they were trespassing. She had had to get permission from the owner before she could use the wood. Seconds later they were flying over the meadow towards the cottages and the call box. Sindy saw Mrs. Martin getting her washing in. When Mrs. Martin looked up Sindy gave her a wave. Soon Sindy's manor house would come into view.

"That's it over there!" yelled Sindy.

"The one with the men on the roof?" Travis replied.

Travis was right. There were two men on the roof. There was also one in the drive looking around on the ground close to a big transit van.

"My goodness!" yelled Sindy.

"Anything wrong?" asked the pilot.

"They are about to break into my house! I

knew I should have called the police!"

"You mean they are thieves?"

"They must be! Can't we land and stop them?"

"I think I know how to deter them! I hope they are crooks and not workmen!" Travis banked the micro light, dipped its nose and flew straight for the roof.

Sindy could see the horrified looks on the two men's faces. Both scrambled to get onto the ladder. The one looking around on the ground suddenly looked up to see the micro light skim the roof top, and his two companions falling along with the ladder. Meanwhile the micro light flew along the lane just above the tree tops, before turning towards the new by-pass.

"Ah! There they are in their usual spot," shouted Travis.

Sindy looked ahead and saw the parked police car. Suddenly she realised that they were landing on the by-pass.

The two policemen leapt out of their car and came running over. They wanted to know what was going on.

"You tell them, Sindy! I'm taking off while the road is clear! See you back at the airfield!"

While the micro light was taking off, Sindy was explaining to one of the policemen the reason for the surprise landing. She told him about the two men on her roof. "I'm sure they were trying to break-in!"

The control room at the police station was informed of a suspected break-in and that the car making the call was on its way to investigate.

The crook who had been looking around in the drive was helping his limping mates into the van when the squad car arrived. In the house Sindy could hear Rufus barking. Sindy opened the front door and let him out. It was just as well the rascals had been thwarted from breaking-in in the usual manner by the locks on Sindy's doors and windows. One of the constables explained to Sindy that no house is one hundred per cent burglar proof. As a last resort if they are determined to get in, they will go through the roof. "You must have quite a bit worth pinching, miss! I wonder how they came to know about it?"

Sindy said she thought she knew. She told them about the well groomed visitor who had

called that morning.

"It would seem that the big fish have given us the slip, miss!" said one of the constables. "These three would appear to be small time crooks. I doubt very much if they know where the ring leaders are!"

Sindy remembered the big white car in the wood and told the constable.

"It's worth following up, miss!" he replied, and leaving his companion to deal with the other three, set off with Sindy and her dog in the police car.

The couple were still sunning themselves when Sindy, Rufus, and the policeman appeared. Yes, it was the same white Rolls Royce that had glided into Sindy's drive that morning, but the couple looked different.

They were very indignant at being disturbed. According to them they were not trespassing, they were friends of the owner. They had been there the best part of the day picnicking and swimming. Both denied having ever seen Sindy before.

That the girl had been swimming there was no denying, but there was still a faint trace of the very strong perfume. It was Rufus who broke the deadlock, when he started sniffing at the crumbs on the car rug spread on the ground. Close by was the girl's hand bag. In her haste to snatch it up some of the contents fell out, one of them being the other tear drop earring. The girl went pale when Sindy produced the other from her pocket.

"Where did you get it?" she snapped.

"I was about to ask you the same question," Sindy replied. "The last time I saw these earrings, until you arrived this morning, they were adorning the ears of a fond aunt of mine!"

Onto the scene arrived a peppery gentleman in tweeds carrying a shot gun. It was the owner of the wood. He demanded to know what was going on. Were the couple friends of his? He was acquainted with Miss Sindy but he had never set eyes on the other two before. He demanded the constable arrest them for trespassing. If the constable wouldn't drive them down to the police station he would march them down at gun point. The couple had no option. They departed in the police car bitterly complaining about wrongful arrest. The land owner went with them to make sure there was no nonsense.

Sindy was left with Rufus and the big white car. Sindy looked in the boot of the car. Bundled in a grip were the expensive clothes her visitor had been wearing that morning. Another police car arrived just as Sindy was thinking of leaving. They had come to collect the Rolls as well as Sindy. She had the choice of riding in either vehicle. Sindy chose the Rolls. It is not every day that she gets a chance to ride in one.

"Thanks to you, Miss Sindy," said the police inspector, "we seem to have hit the jackpot with these two. They are wanted in just about every county in the country for robbery!"

Sindy wondered if that was how the girl came to be wearing her aunt's earrings.

The inspector offered her the telephone. "If you know her telephone number why not ring her and find out?"

Aunt Lucy was very surprised to hear her favourite niece on the 'phone. Had she still got her tear drop earrings? No, they were stolen with a lot of other property when her home was burgled about a year ago.

"Can I come and see you, Aunt Lucy?" Sindy enquired.

Aunt Lucy would be only too delighted if she did. Yes, she could bring a young man with her if she wished.

When Sindy arrived home she found Glenda waiting with her Range Rover in the drive. She had heard from Dave Travis about the near break-in. She learned the rest from Sindy over a pot of tea.

"How did you like flying in his micro light?" Glenda asked.

"Super!" Sindy replied. "He doesn't know it yet but he is taking me up again this weekend!"

Aunt Lucy was delighted to see Sindy again. She was also delighted with Dave's micro light and insisted on a flight. Sindy handed her the earrings and told her of the part the young pilot had played in retrieving them.

Aunt Lucy beamed.

"They are not mine anymore, Sindy! They are yours! You'd have had them before only they were stolen! You can't wear big earrings when you wear a crash helmet. Come and see my new motor bike!"

Uncle Owen joined Sindy to watch the micro light take off.

"She is just as scatty as ever, Sindy," he sighed. "What is the betting she gives up riding motor bikes and takes up flying micro lights?"

"She really is my giddy aunt," laughed Sindy.

A few days later Sindy met Glenda again. They talked about the attempted break-in. One thing puzzled Sindy, however. How did the well groomed visitor know who she was? Glenda laughed.

"There are very few people who don't know who you are, Sindy!"

Sindy's Show-Jumping Game

Instead of a horse all you need is a dice and a counter per player to enter this great show-jumping competition with all the thrills and spills of the show-jumping ring — and you don't even need to know how to ride a horse to enjoy playing this game. As in real show-jumping, the rider with the minimum number of faults is the winner.

If you land on these squares...

Move on to the next blue square.

4 faults.

Horse refuses. Go back 3 squares. 4 faults.

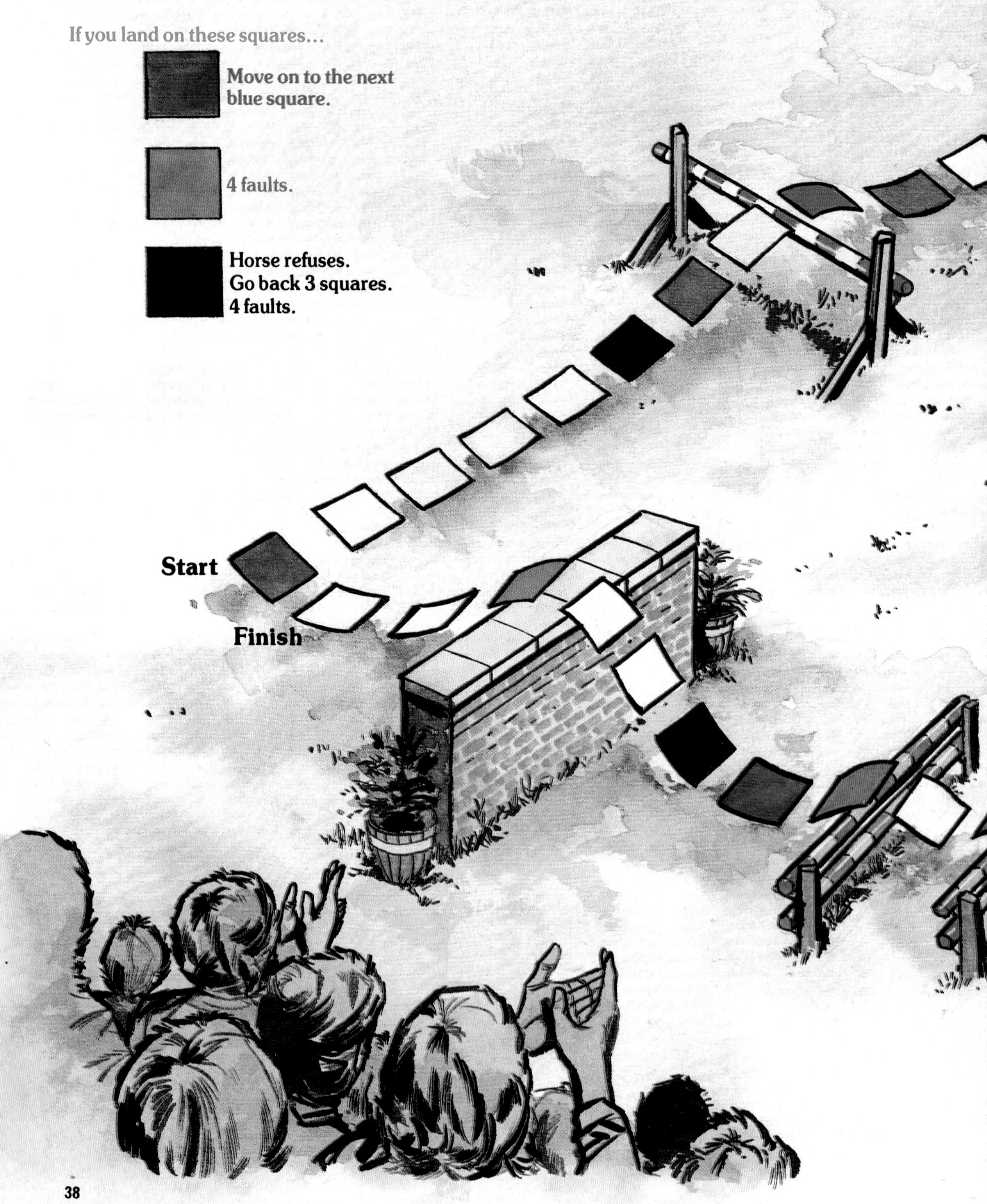

You can also have a 'jump-off against the clock'. For this you will need a watch or a clock with a second hand. The rider who finishes the course in the shortest time with the least number of faults is the winner..

Sindy Keeps Slim And Trim

Once there was nothing I liked better than to put my feet up and watch TV or to play records or read my favourite magazine! Then someone told me I was lazy and unfit — and that did it! Mind you, it wasn't easy getting me out of my chair at first, but I'm glad now that I've changed my ways.

Being fit and healthy is an important part of looking good (no, I didn't believe it for a while either!). Having nice skin and hair and clothes isn't everything.

"But I hate exercise," I wailed to my friend, "especially when it's cold!" But I don't have to wait for summer to come along anymore. And, do you know, I have such a lot of fun now and have made lots of new friends. What's more — it hardly costs me anything.

To let you into a secret, I used to love eating all the 'wrong' things. Mmmm! Burger and chips, crisps, chocolate bars, cakes and big sandwiches oozing with jam! Luckily my tastes changed before it was too late and now I like savoury things much more, and they are generally much more healthy to eat.

Part one of my plan was to change my diet. I told my mum to stop giving me fattening things like I've mentioned, even if I screamed! She agreed with my friend that a sensible eating plan was the best thing for me, and we worked it out together. Slowly I stopped taking sugar in tea and coffee, and I started to eat only half the bread and potatoes that I used to. I can't help loving butter, but these days I treat myself to a little bit rather than big, thick blobs!

Mum said that jacket and boiled potatoes were much less fattening than chips, and I'm happy because at least I can still eat them!

Now I hardly ever nibble sweets, biscuits, cakes or crisps. Instead I eat some fruit or raw carrots and celery and sometimes a piece of cheese. Milkshakes and fizzy drinks are out, too! I make sure that I drink lots of water which also makes my skin look great. The last time I went to the dentist, guess what? "No fillings," he said. I was thrilled to bits!

I don't believe in strict diets — and I've proved that I can still eat a lot without becoming fat. My rules are three meals a day — a boiled egg and toast for breakfast, lots of fish and lean meat and vegetables, salad and fruit. I asked Mum to be a bit more adventurous at meal times and she was pleased! After all, she was getting fed up with cooking peas and cabbage — and the recipe books had us both dribbling!

Part two of the new regime, as I said, was to start keeping fit. I got my bicycle from under the cobwebs in the garden shed and *used* it. When I don't ride to (or with) my friends, I walk to the shops or wherever. Why be lazy and take the bus if you don't have to? I learned to swim at school, so I was lucky, but if I hadn't, I would have found a pool to learn in with my friends. I go each week and swim plenty of widths. (And I take a couple of apples to eat afterwards... I'm always starving!)

Joining in some more of the games lessons at school, is another way of getting regular exercise and who knows you may even end up finding out you're fantastic at running or gym, netball or tennis. I like to jog round the garden or round the local park. It's a chance to wear my favourite tracksuits, too.

But apart from the 'outdoor' type of exercise, I've found a great way of keeping fit, especially when it's cold, raining or dark. My friends and I go to each others' houses and dance or do exercises, both to music, of course! It's fantastic... we can listen to our favourite records, keep fit *and* have a laugh at the same time. The Green Goddess has nothing on us!

Don't get me wrong... I still love to sit around, and I'm *not* perfect! I love chips and chocolate, but now I like them much better as a real 'treat'. My spending money lasts longer and what's more, I have lots more energy then I used to. I feel much happier with the way I look, the way I am... trim, healthy and ready to get up and go!

So go on — get out your skipping rope, start to enjoy fresh air and jump for joy! Good luck!

Sindy Finds The Cure

Production meetings at the t.v. studios were apt to drag on right through the lunch hour which was why Sindy stopped off at 'The Coffee Pot' to pick up some sandwiches. She could hear peals of laughter from within as she parked her scooter. She wondered whatever was going on. As she was about to enter she was nearly sent spinning by a young nurse who came dashing out.

"Ooops! Sorry, luv!" gasped the nurse, stopping Sindy from falling. A big smile of recognition came over the girl's face.

"You're Sindy, aren't you?" she beamed. Before Sindy could answer she was off down the street calling over her shoulder that it was nice bumping into her and that she was sorry she could not stop but she had to get back.

They were still rolling about with laughter when Sindy entered the cafe.

"Morning, Miss Sindy!" said Joe, the proprietor, wiping a tear from his eye. "You just missed a good laugh! That nurse who was in here! She should be in show business. Everytime she comes here she has us in stitches! She's a born comedienne if I ever saw one, and I've met a few in my time!"

"It's a pity you missed her," said the girl wiping the tables. Sindy was on the point of telling them that she hadn't when she spotted the carrier bag by the counter.

"It's hers!" said the girl. "I'd better go after her!"

"I'll go," replied Sindy, picking up the bag. "I've got my scooter outside. I'll be right back for my sandwiches!"

Had Sindy not been held up by the traffic lights she would have caught up with the nurse long before she got to the hospital. She arrived in time to see her dash through the entrance of the Casualty Department. Sindy parked her scooter and hurried in after her. As she entered, a young man clad in motor cycling leathers was coming out. He stopped Sindy to show her his bandaged hand.

"I came off and hurt my wrist," he said with a bit of a grin. "What happened to you?"

"Er-nothing!" replied Sindy, who did not wish to appear rude. "I hope your wrist gets better soon-er-now if you will excuse me!"

A young doctor appeared from behind a screen. He took one look at Sindy in her riding outfit and crash helmet and sighed. "Not another biker! You're the fifth this morning! Let's take a look at you!"

"I'm not a casualty," Sindy explained, "although it's a wonder I didn't become one when one of your nurses cannoned into me!"

She then told the doctor her reason for being where she was, and offered him the carrier bag. The doctor peered in at the contents and then called a nurse over.

"Nurse Digby has been on one of her errands of mercy again, nurse!" he said.

Sindy looked surprised. The doctor then explained.

"Nurse Digby will do anything for the kids on her ward. If they haven't got what they want at the hospital shop she slips out and gets it elsewhere. It's strictly against the rules, and she knows she'll be for it if she is caught!"

"Would you be so good as to see that she gets it? Sindy asked the nurse.

"No way," said the nurse. "I'm not risking running into Sister Figgis!"

"Don't look at me," the young doctor said. "Figgis and I don't quite see eye to eye."

He then suggested that the nurse give the ward a ring, and if the coast was clear that Sindy might take it up via the service lift. There was no reply. According to the doctor that was a good sign. If nobody was in the office, Sister Figgis was off the ward.

It was Sindy's intention to slip up quickly and leave the bag, but things did not quite work out that way. As she stepped out of the lift someone was waiting to step into it. A small pyjama clad lad with a bandaged head, clutching a teddy bear. Sindy knew that he should not be there.

"And where might you be off to, young man?" she enquired.

He was off home to see his Mum. She had not been in to see him so he was going home to see *her*.

Sindy thought hard and fast. She did not want any tears or fuss.

"Don't you think you ought to get dressed first?" she asked.

He informed Sindy that he could not dress himself and asked Sindy if she would help him. Sindy replied that she might, and suggested that he guide her to the ward so they could get them. Sindy breathed a sigh of relief when he clasped her hand and lead her solomnly along the corridor. As they approached the office, Sindy heard voices raised within.

"I haven't got eyes in the back of my head," said one.

"You haven't got any in front either," the other replied. "You should have left the door open when you were 'phoning!"

"I don't want everyone listening to my conversation, especially you!"

"We've got to find young Jimmy before Figgis gets back, or it's goodbye to our nursing careers!"

"Yours. Not mine! You're the one she left in charge!"

"This isn't my day! First I lose the kids' shopping only to come back to find one of them missing! Go into the ward while I take another look for him!"

"Is this the young man you are looking for?" asked Sindy, ushering her charge into the office. "I found him by the service lift when I was returning your shopping!"

For a moment the two nurses stood speechless.

"It's Jimmy!" screeched the young trainee nurse.

"Look who is with him!" exclaimed Nurse Digby. "It's Sindy!"

She could not thank Sindy enough. Sindy informed her that it was the doctor in Casualty that she ought to thank.

"Good old Smithy! Pity he was switched to Casualty. The kids certainly miss him!" she said, and invited Sindy to meet the kids and help hand out the goodies while Nurse Pomfrey put young Jimmy back in his bed.

"Thanks," replied Sindy, "but I really must be going. I promise I'll call in some time when I'm not so busy!"

Sindy was destined to stay. Jimmy did not want Pomfrey to put him to bed. He wanted Sindy.

"Promise you will stay there if I do!" said Sindy. Little Jimmy nodded and lead her into the ward and towards his bed.

"Hey, kids!" called Nurse Digby. "We've got a very special visitor. Do you know who she is?"

"Yes!" chorused the ward. "SINDY!"

"Do you know who Sindy is, Gertie Gigglepot?" the nurse asked a small giggling miss in one of the beds.

"Yeth!" she lisped, and went into fits of giggles.

They all knew Sindy and her 'Pop Spot' show, and also because she sometimes told stories on one of the children's programmes.

They expected Sindy to tell them one right there and then, until Nurse Digby told them that Sindy was busy putting Jimmy back to bed, and then she must leave.

"You tell us one then," they cried. "That funny one about the dancing Egyptian princess!"

The whole ward was soon in an uproar as Nurse Digby did her version of the old music hall sand dance. The café proprietor was right. Nurse Digby indeed was a born comedienne. Sindy would have liked to have stayed for the whole performance but she was already late for her production meeting. After promising Jimmy that she would be back to visit him, she slipped quietly out of the ward. The sound of the laughing children followed her down the corridor. She could still hear them when she entered the lift.

"Did you bump into Sister Figgis?" asked the young doctor, as she was passing. It was just as well Sindy had not. He had heard through the hospital 'grape vine' that Sister Figgis was not in a good mood. She had just had a stormy encounter with one of the senior consultants.

After the fun on the ward, Sindy found the production meeting that morning quite boring. What a pity Nurse Digby wasn't there. She would have livened things up. The only thing that interested Sindy was the suggestion put up by someone that they do a talent spotting show, but the idea was turned down because a rival company already had one. The meeting over, Sindy spent the rest of the day getting her next 'Pop Spot' programme together. She thought she would pay a quick promised visit to little Jimmy at the hospital before returning home to her flat.

The ward seemed very subdued when she entered. No peals of laughter like there were that morning. Nurse Digby was not around. She assumed that she was off duty.

It was a different sister who spoke to Sindy. She knew she could not possibly be Sister Figgis. This one was very friendly, and was very pleased that Sindy could find time to visit young Jimmy. The reason that his mother did not come was because she was in the hospital, too. Both had been involved in a road accident. Sindy offered to look in when she could until Jimmy's mother was fit enough to take over.

On leaving the hospital, Sindy met up with the young doctor she had met that morning. He asked Sindy if she had heard the bad news.

"What bad news?" asked Sindy.

Nurse Digby had been dismissed. She had left the hospital that afternoon.

Sindy and the young doctor wandered along to the 'Coffee Pot'. Bad news travels fast. They knew of her dismissal, too. She had called in to say goodbye before catching a train for the North.

"We're going to miss her," said Joe the proprietor.

"Not as much as the kids," the young doctor replied.

"We may not have seen the last of her," said Joe. "I gave her the address of a pal of

mine who is in show business up North to look up if she wished!"

"It's a pity she did not come and see me," said Sindy.

Over their meal, Sindy learned what had happened. When Sister Figgis returned from her stormy meeting with the senior consultant she caught Debbie Digby doing her act. She was not amused to find the nurse imitating her.

"No sense of humour, that woman," said the young doctor.

"Surely that was not all she was dismissed for," said Sindy.

"Not quite," the doctor replied. "She had spotted Digby slipping out when she was in the senior consultant's office where she was getting a wigging for sending him the wrong x-rays. Digby got the blame for that, too, although I suspect it was Nurse Pomfrey who was responsible, even though Digby never let on!"

It was over a week before Sindy had the chance to visit the hospital again. She had been sent on an assignment abroad. All the kids were pleased to see her, especially young Jimmy. As she was leaving she realised the little girl, 'Gertie Gigglepot' was not on the ward. Had she recovered? Quite the opposite. She had been removed to a side ward. According to the nurse, her health, for no apparent reason, had deteriorated, and the operation they had been building her up for had to be put off.

It was a sad little face that looked up at Sindy from between the sheets. She gave Sindy a faint smile and with a whispered lisp asked for 'Nurth Digby'.

"That's all she seems to say," said the nurse.

"Do you think it might help if she came back just to see her?" Sindy asked.

"It might," the nurse replied. "I think Nurse Pomfrey suggested it and got her head bitten off by Sister Figgis for her pains! Anyway, nobody knows where Debbie Digby is."

Sindy thought the proprietor of the 'Coffee Pot' might. By the time she arrived the cafe was closed. Sindy returned to her flat, cooked herself some supper and sat and watched t.v. She chose a channel at random, and the programme she saw was the talent spotting show that had been discussed at the production meeting.

The act she saw was quite corny. She was about to switch channels when the presenter introduced the next act, Miss Cleo Patra. The girl Sindy saw was dressed like an ancient Egyptian princess. She was poised like a figure on a frieze. The audience were already laughing before she started her dance. There was no doubt about it. The girl was Debbie Digby. She had them rolling in the aisles when she started her sand dance.

There was no sleep for Sindy that night. She drove her Range Rover up the motorway.

It was gone mid-night when she arrived at the studios. The audience and performers had long gone. She was told by one of the night staff that she was not the only one after Miss Cleo Patra. The switch board had been jammed with calls since her performance.

"I bet the guy who got her onto the show is celebrating his luck tonight," said the young man.

"Do you happen to know who he is?" asked Sindy.

The young man did, and warned that she would have to queue to see him at his office after the girl's performance.

Sindy drove her Range Rover round to the agent's office. She made sure that she'd be the first to see him.

He knew Sindy but she did not know him. "It's going to cost you a packet to get her on your show, Sindy!" he said gleefully. "This young lady is going places with me!"

Sindy asked him if he would be so kind as to let her know where she might find Debbie Digby. The wily agent would not let on. Sindy noticed the contract on his desk.

"Now if you will kindly wait outside with the others until she arrives," he said.

Sindy said that she would only be too delighted. She recognised one or two of the people waiting in the outer office. She strolled outside and waited by her Range Rover. Sindy was the first person Debbie Digby saw when she arrived at the agent's office.

"Gosh! You of all people, Sindy! Did you see me on the box last night?" she exclaimed.

Sindy congratulated her on her performance, and then told her her reason for driving up through the night.

"Poor little Gertie!" the ex-nurse exclaimed. "Let's get going right away!"

"What about signing your contract?" Sindy asked.

"He said he'd been waiting a long time for someone like me to come along. So he can wait a big longer! Will you drive or shall I?" she replied climbing into the Range Rover.

On the way down Debbie Digby thought she might know why Gertie was behaving like she was.

"That poor kid has had quite a few ops already. Each one has been a flop. I told her that this one would be different if I came and held her hand."

No sooner did Debbie Digby step into the side ward than the little girl began to smile. In a matter of minutes she was starting to giggle. In stormed Sister Figgis followed by the senior consultant. Sister Figgis was livid. She ordered both Sindy and Debbie Digby out. The consultant told them to stay.

"But this is Digby, Sir! The girl I had dismissed! She is too irresponsible to nurse

anyone let alone sick children," she screeched.

"She seems to be responsible for that child's recovery," the senior consultant replied. "We cannot delay the operation much longer.

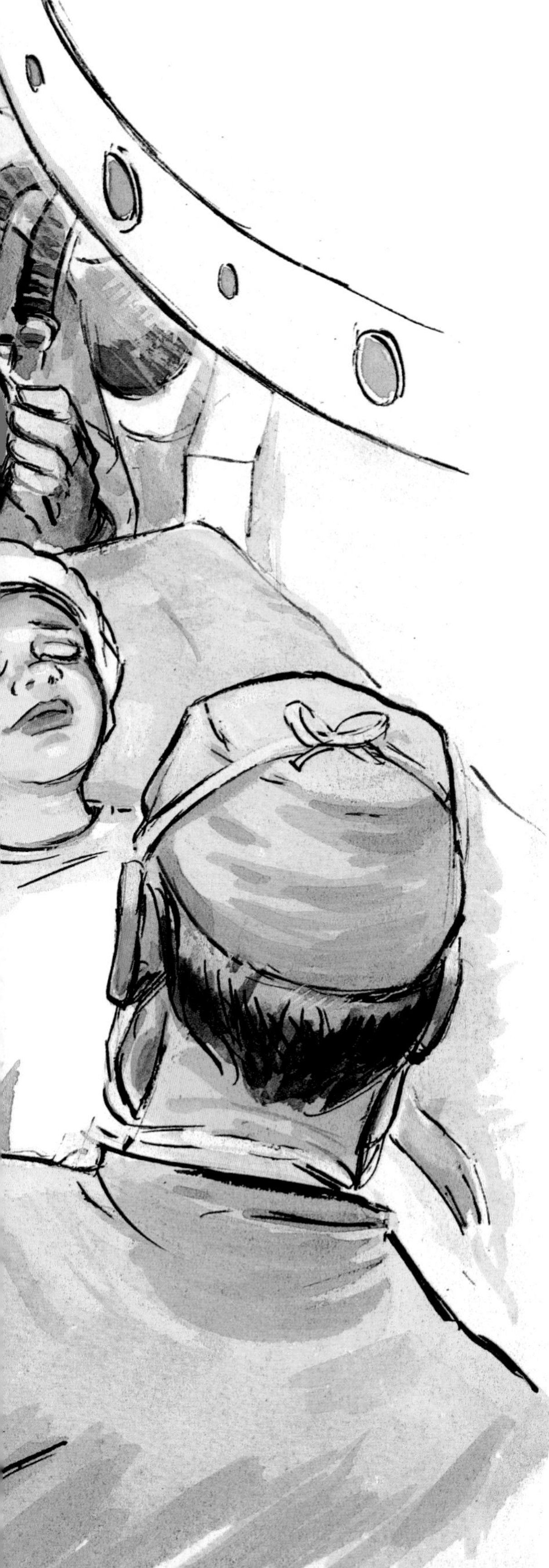

The young ladies may stay for as along as they wish to do so!"

"Hooray!" piped small voices in the corridor.

Sister Figgis nearly threw a fit when she saw the happy faces round the door. "Back to bed all of you!" she screamed. Nobody made a move.

"Off to bed you lot," said Debbie Digby. "I'll send Sindy in in a minute! Last one into bed is a weed!"

They couldn't get back into the ward quick enough.

Meanwhile, thinking Sindy had tricked him, the agent travelled down from the North. He got short shift from Debbie Digby when he called at the hospital.

"Don't judge everyone by your own standards," she said. "If they will take me back nursing then the waste paper bin is the only place for your contract!"

The agent pleaded with Sindy. "Tell her she is crazy! She is throwing away a brilliant career!"

Sindy agreed, but Debbie Digby was adamant. No way was she going anywhere until the child had had her operation and recovered.

'Gertie Gigglepot', had her op. As promised the ex-nurse went with her into the operating theatre, and stayed by her bedside until she knew she was on the road to recovery. When not at the hospital she stayed with Sindy in her flat.

One evening she told Sindy that 'Gertie' had recovered enough to go home and that her parents would be coming to fetch her.

"Does that mean you are going to start out again on your new career?" asked Sindy.

"No," she replied. "I am going back to my old one. Kindly address me as Sister in future!"

Sister Figgis had decided to leave. Debbie Digby had applied for the post and had been given the job.

However she was to appear on t.v. again when Sindy brought her 'Pop Spot' show onto the ward, and thanks to Sister Digby's antics, the show was an enormous success, so much so that it won an award for 'the best light entertainment' show of the year.

Sindy continued to visit the ward long after young Jimmy's mother had recovered enough to come and see him.

Debbie Digby had other offers to turn professional but no amount of money could tempt the would be zany star off her ward where she said she had a captive audience who could not get out of bed and switch her off.

Sindy's Pop Gossip

Kim Wilde:

If there is one thir the beautiful Kim Wilc to avoid . . . it's not her but trees! "A favourite hobby of mine is skiing, she says. "So I always t and take a winter holida can. I never like to go alc but always with a bunch c friends, many of whom I was at school with and still keep in touch with.

"But much as I love skiing, I nearly always find myself heading at speed towards a tree as I race along the slopes. Once I nearly went flat, and I get so many bruises . . . but it's all worth it!" And about those friends of hers . . . she keeps all their photographs on the walls of her flat!

Heaven 17:

Glen Gregory of 'Heaven 17' likes to be prepared for when he gets inspiration to write a new song for the group. "So I keep a piano in my bedroom," he says. "Many's the time I've been up in the early hours of the morning composing. Luckily my wife's a songwriter too so she understands."

He also has a dog which, he says: "I love to take to the shops with me. He runs round people's legs and creates havoc. I'm almost embarrassed sometimes."

The Thompson Twins:

In most countries in the world, 'The Thompson Twins', Alannah Currie, Tom Bailey and Joe Leeway would be mobbed by fans. "But in France, nobody seems to know who we are," says Tom. "It's quite good really, because when we go there to record an album we get some privacy." But it can also have its bad moments. "When we want to go to a classy restaurant, we're often refused entry because they don't like the way we dress." Keep a watch out for Tom. It's not all jet plane travel for him. "I love riding on ordinary buses," he says.

Paul King: King:

Paul King, who is leader of the colourful group, 'King', started off in life as an actor. But when he left drama college he found himself doing some rather unusual jobs. "One of them," he says, "was as a monk. Not a real one, but I had to pretend to be like one for fun. The job was in a huge house where they held mock medieval banquets for people. They'd come along for a meal and everyone would be in fancy dress of the time. I had to chat to them all and it was marvellous."

ahl:

Limahl knew that he ...nted to be an entertainer ...n the moment that he ...ld walk.

"I used to sing ...ywhere," he says. "My ...ourite places were record ...ops. I'd go in whilst ...ople were buying albums ...d jump up on the counter ...nd perform a few numbers ...r them." He also sang to ...rowds and queues ...herever he could find ...hem. No wonder he can ...andle an audience so well ...ow!

Imagination:

'Imagination' have sold millions of records around the world, but they reckon that nothing compares for excitement with the prospect of playing Russia! "We went to Poland for a series of concerts," says lead singer, Leee John, "and whilst we were there we made a film documentary for them which is to be shown right across the Iron Curtain countries. Hopefully, it'll mean we might be doing concerts in the Soviet Union." Meanwhile, Leee's favourite pastime is reading film books. "I want the group to go into films as the next stage and do comedy stuff like the Marx brothers," he says.

...ythmics:

Most group members ...e within easy reach of one ...nother, if they don't share ...ats or whatever. But Annie ...ennox and Dave Stewart ...of 'Eurythmics' are miles ...away. Annie lives in Switzerland whilst Dave is in London. "It's really beautiful there," she says, "and not far from the mountains." When they want to record they usually go to Paris and shut themselves away for weeks to write their songs. Annie also loves dressing up for her videos and has a huge collection of wigs as any fan of the group must have realised!

Ultravox:

Midge Ure of 'Ultravox' is a guy with an ambition to make films. "I don't think I can be a pop star forever," he says. "So I'm trying to learn the art of directing and acting in films. I've already got a few ideas up my sleeve and maybe the whole group'll be involved." Meanwhile, he has had a recording studio built at the bottom of his garden. "It means that whenever I get an idea for a song I can just nip down the garden and record it," he says.

Zoe Bates
– a bright new show-jumping star

Zoe Bates is a really exciting show jumper who has won loads of prizes competing in events all around Europe. Recently she was given the 'Young Show-Jumper of The Future Award'. I went along to have a chat with her about her horses and the competitions she enters, to find out something about her life. And I think you'll agree that she is a really interesting person!

Sindy: Tell me, Zoe, have you always been surrounded by horses or was your first pony a birthday present?
Zoe: My mother was a show-jumper and my father was a steeplechase jockey. But the funny thing was that neither of them went to watch the other compete because neither found it exciting. I was lucky because I went and watched both of them. So we always had horses at home.
Sindy: Did you live on a farm, then?
Zoe: Not at first. We lived in a house with quite a bit of land, but then a motorway was built near us and Dad couldn't keep the horses there any more. So we moved to our present home, which is a farm.
Sindy: How many horses do you own now?
Zoe: About ten. They need an awful lot of looking after. But I'm lucky in that I've got a girl groom who helps me a lot and she travels with me when I have to go abroad to take part in competitions.
Sindy: Are the horses expensive to buy?
Zoe: Yes. They cost an awful lot of money, especially a good showjumping horse. So what I do, is to buy young horses and then train them up myself. It's a lot more work, but then it's the only way that I could afford to do it, especially with the enormous bill for feeding all of the animals, and the replacement of the necessary riding equipment. That's not to mention all of the travelling expenses that I have to pay when I go anywhere, especially abroad!
Sindy: Where exactly have you been out of this country?
Zoe: I've been to France lots of times. Then Belgium, Switzerland, Holland, Norway and Germany. I've not been to America because it is so difficult trying to transport the horses over such a long distance . . . and expensive too.
Sindy: What about language difficulties, then, when you travel?
Zoe: Well, I do speak fluent French, but that wasn't because I was good at it at school. In fact I was pretty useless there. It was just travelling to France so much I had to learn it to survive. Like what to eat, directions, instructions for the competitions and things like that!
Sindy: So when you do go abroad, how do you take the horse? Does it travel separately?
Zoe: Oh, no! I always go with the horse. I've got this lorry which I drive myself, and it's tremendous fun. It's also got all modern conveniences in it like a shower, bed and kitchen facilities.
Sindy: That sounds exciting. I'll have to try and get one of those for myself! Isn't it difficult driving the lorry, though. Not many girls do that, do they?
Zoe: I guess not. But then I've been brought up with this way of life. When I was very young I used to travel with my mother when she went to competitions all around the country. My mother drove the lorry and I used to sit in the driving cab with her. We were always breaking down on motorways or in out-of-the-way places and having to try and mend the lorry ourselves. It was a lot of fun, and I always promised myself that when I was old enough, I'd drive myself around in a lorry too.
Sindy: Has anything exciting ever happened to you when you've been travelling?
Zoe: There was one occasion when I was driving home in England and I was stopped by the police who thought that I was a cattle rustler. It was quite amusing really . . . it made me feel like someone out of one of those Western movies. They were quite apologetic when they realised I was a show-jumper.
Sindy: Have you ever had to take your horse on a boat?
Zoe: Yes, I have. When I wanted to drive to an event in Norway.
Sindy: I should imagine that it isn't all that easy. Doesn't the horse get frightened?
Zoe: If you aren't careful it can. When I went to Norway it was an overnight crossing. What is important is that you make certain that the back of the lorry is down so that the horse can breathe properly. But the problem is that the captain of the ship and the crew don't like the back of the lorry down. I had an awkward time trying to explain it had to be that way for the safety of the horse.
Sindy: They did understand you, then?
Zoe: Well, it sounds a bit mischievous, but whilst miming to the man and pulling the lorry back down, it fell on

Zoe at the wheel of the lorry she uses to drive herself to competitions throughout Europe.

his head. I wanted to laugh but didn't dare. He wasn't hurt. Just surprised!

Sindy: What do other girl riders abroad think of you when you drive up in your lorry?

Zoe: They're a bit shocked, because in other countries girls never ever travel with their horses. They just turn up at events and ride them. I think it is because the British have a love of all animals.

Sindy: Do you have any other animals?

Zoe: I used to have some pet monkeys at home once. They were really lovely. And also a sheep which was just like a dog. I could call to it out of my bedroom window and it would come running to me. Once when my mother was away at a competition a bird flew into my bedroom and built a nest in my curtains. I loved it, but my mother wasn't too pleased. I also kept mice when I was at boarding school. We used to keep them in our pockets.

Sindy: When did you first win a major competition?

Zoe: That was in 1980 when I represented Britain at the Junior European Championships. Then I went on to the Junior Nations' Cup Team in France and also the Grand Prix in France.
I won the gold medal at the next attempt in the Junior European Championships with the British team in Switzerland and the Grand Prix in Belgium. And since

then I've had a nice string of wins.
Sindy: You also won the award for the Young Show-jumper of the Future, so have you ever been to a fortune teller to find out if you'll win a competition?
Zoe: I did once, when I was in France. She told me that I was going to win. Well I went in for the major event and didn't, so I felt that she'd been wrong. But straight after I went in this little event and won, so maybe she was thinking of that!
Sindy: Are you superstitious about anything before you go into a riding competition?
Zoe: I think most people are about something. In my case, if I've accidentally put on an item of clothing inside out, then I won't put it on the right way. I'll just go out and compete like it.
Sindy: Has anything amusing happened to you at a competition?
Zoe: I was once invited out by some important people to dinner. When they asked me I was covered in mud because I'd just finished riding. I rushed to change and on my way I discovered that although I was wearing a beautiful dress, in my hurry I was still wearing these filthy wellington boots.
Sindy: What would you like to achieve now?
Zoe: I'd like to become the top show-jumper in the country and also continue to enjoy building up young horses into great competition winners!

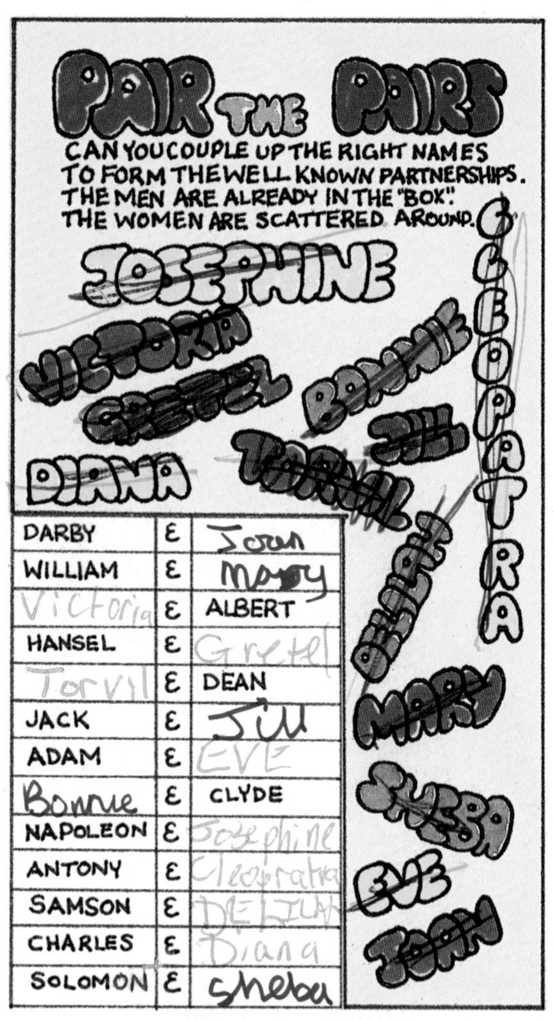

DARBY	&	
WILLIAM	&	
	&	ALBERT
HANSEL	&	
	&	DEAN
JACK	&	
ADAM	&	
	&	CLYDE
NAPOLEON	&	
ANTONY	&	
SAMSON	&	
CHARLES	&	
SOLOMON	&	

GIRLS IN A WHIRL

HOW MANY GIRLS' NAMES CAN YOU FIND IN THIS PUZZLE?

JANETHELMARIANNANCYNTHIANDREAUGUSTACYVONNELLINDAPHNEVELYNETTESSARAHILDAISYBILYDIANADIANTHEATHERICATHLEENORMABELLAGNESTELLAMBERYLUCYOLLANDELIANTONIALICELIAPRILAURACHELENATALIELSAMANTHANNAOMIONELIZABETHORA

GIRLS IN THE GARDEN

CAN YOU FIND OUT HOW MANY, AND NAME THEM?

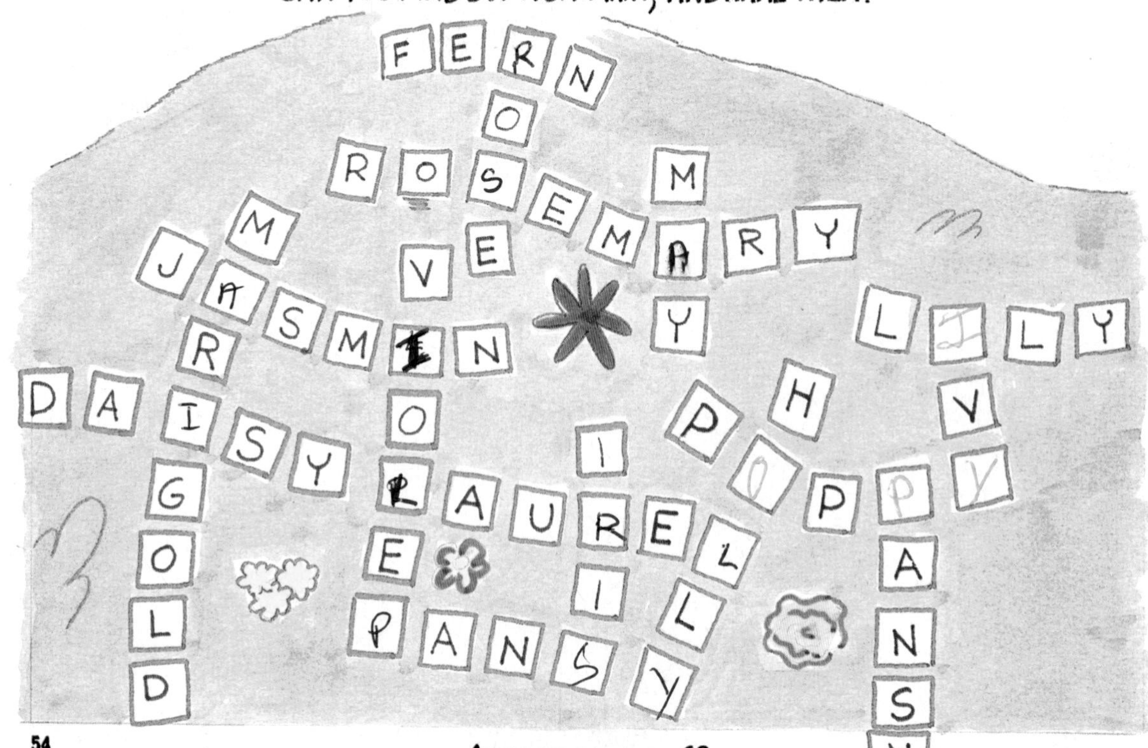

Answers on page 63.

Sindy takes a hand

IT WAS BY FAR AND AWAY THE BEST HISTORICAL PAGEANT THAT EVER WOUND ITS WAY THROUGH THE NARROW STREETS OF CASTLEBRIDGE, THANKS MAINLY TO THE YOUNG LADY WHO LIVED IN HER MANOR HOUSE NOT FAR FROM THE LITTLE ANCIENT TOWN. LITTLE DID THE CHEERING TOWNSFOLK KNOW WHAT A PROBLEM IT HAD BEEN FOR SINDY, THE DAY BEFORE, WHEN SHE HAD TO COME TO THE AID OF THE LOCAL BROWNIES, AND SORT OUT THE PROBLEM OF THE TWO "GOOD QUEEN BESSES"...

MOST OF THE PROBLEMS HAD BEEN IRONED OUT BY THE PREVIOUS AFTERNOON, OR SO SINDY THOUGHT AS SHE GROOMED HER HORSE...

???

BE SO GOOD AS TO INFORM YOUR EMPLOYER THAT I WISH TO SEE HER!

WHO SHALL I SAY'S CALLING?

MISS THELMA HARCOURT OF HARCOURT HALL!

WHAT CAN I DO FOR YOU, MISS HARCOURT? I'M SINDY! I PRESUME IT'S ME YOU WISH TO SEE!
HAW! HAW! YOU PLONKED YOUR HOOF IN THAT TIME, THELMA!
FANCY! I TOOK YOU TO BE HER STABLE MAID!
THELMA HARCOURT INFORMED SINDY OF THE REASON FOR HER CALL...
I'M AFRAID YOU HAVE LEFT IT A BIT LATE! WE ALREADY HAVE A GOOD QUEEN BESS ENTERED!
THEN TELL HER TO COME AS SOMEONE ELSE! IT'S COST DADDY A PACKET TO HIRE MY COSTUME AND THOSE FOR MY COURTIERS!

AND WHEN SINDY REFUSED...
VERY WELL! TELL ME WHO SHE IS AND I WILL TELL HER MYSELF!
NO!
TRY COMING AS AN HAWAIIAN DANCER—THAT WON'T COST YOUR FATHER SO MUCH!
WHAT A SUPER IDEA!
SHUT UP! IF SHE WON'T TELL ME, I KNOW SOMEONE WHO WILL!
SINDY WENT BACK TO HER GROOMING...
IT'S JUST AS WELL I DIDN'T TELL HER! SHE'D MAKE MINCEMEAT OF POOR HEATHER!
HEATHER JENKINS WAS BUSY ON THE CHECK OUT AT THE HARCOURT SUPERMARKET WHEN THE OWNER'S DAUGHTER CAME STORMING IN...
IF JACK BRADBURY WISHES TO REMAIN THE MANAGER HE'D BETTER TELL ME!
JACK BRADBURY WAS ALSO ON THE ORGANISING COMMITTEE...
MANAGER
WHERE IS HE? I'LL HAVE HIM HERE AT THE DOUBLE!

SHE WAS ABOUT TO CALL HIM ON THE STORE SPEAKER SYSTEM, WHEN...
HOLD YOUR HORSES, THELMA! WHAT'S THAT UNDER THAT WRAP?
WELL, WELL, WELL! SOMEONE HAS TAKEN A LOT OF TIME AND TROUBLE...
...FOR NOTHING!
GOT THINGS SORTED OUT?
OH, YES! I MOST CERTAINLY HAVE!
IT WAS JUST ON CLOSING TIME WHEN SINDY ARRIVED AT THE STORE...
HELLO, SINDY! I CAN'T WAIT FOR OUR DRESS REHEARSAL! I HOPE HEATHER WON'T BE LONG!
ME, TOO, JILLY! I'VE GOT THE BROWNIES TO SORT OUT AFTER I'VE SEEN TO YOU TWO!
Sindy

I HOPE WE WIN THE HOLIDAY PRIZE! WE'RE GOING TO SEND MUM AND DAD AWAY FOR THEIR ANNIVERSARY PRESENT! DO YOU THINK WE WILL?
YOU DESERVE TO AFTER ALL THE WORK YOUR SISTER HAS PUT IN! HERE SHE COMES NOW!
27p

WHAT'S WRONG WITH HEATHER? WHY IS SHE CRYING?
HEAVENS! LOOK AT THE COSTUME!
WHY SHOULD ANYONE WANT TO DO SUCH A THING, SINDY?
I THINK I KNOW WHY AND WHO DID IT! IF ONLY I HAD PROOF!
CAN IT BE MENDED, SINDY?

SINDY DROVE THE UNHAPPY SISTERS BACK TO HER MANOR HOUSE. THE DRESS WAS TORN BEYOND REPAIR...
THELMA HARCOURT IS NOT GOING TO GET AWAY WITH THIS! IF THAT'S HER PHONING TO GLOAT...!

IT WAS BROWN OWL. ANOTHER PROBLEM FOR SINDY...
I'M SORRY TO HAVE LET YOU DOWN, SINDY!
IT'S NOT YOUR FAULT, BROWN OWL! YOU GO TO BED LIKE THE DOCTOR SAID! DON'T WORRY! I'LL COPE SOMEHOW! I'LL BE OVER TO THE GUIDE HUT AS SOON AS I CAN!
BROWN OWL HAS GONE DOWN WITH FLU! SOME OF THE BROWNIES' OUTFITS STILL HAVE TO BE FINISHED!
IS THERE ANYTHING I CAN DO TO HELP, SINDY!
YES, AND YOU CAN STILL BE IN THE PAGEANT, TOO! COME ON! I'LL EXPLAIN ON THE WAY!
YOU, HEATHER, CAN BE MAID MARIAN INSTEAD OF ME, WHILE I STAND IN FOR BROWN OWL AS ROBIN HOOD!
HEY! WHAT ABOUT ME?
DON'T WORRY, JILLY! WE'LL THINK OF SOMETHING DURING THE EVENING!
SINDY 3
SINDY HAD REALLY GONE TO TOWN WHEN SHE DESIGNED THE COSTUMES FOR THE MERRY MEN...
IF YOU WERE A BROWNIE YOU COULD BE IN THE PAGEANT, TOO!
SINDY HAS PROMISED TO THINK UP SOMETHING AFTER SHE HAS FINISHED WITH YOU LOT!

NEXT MORNING AT THE ASSEMBLY POINT, "GOOD QUEEN BESS" HAD WORDS WITH JACK BRADBURY, THE MANAGER OF HER FATHER'S STORE, AND THE PROCESSION ORGANISER...
THE BROWNIES HAVE YET TO COME AND SO HAS MISS SINDY, MISS HARCOURT!
THAT'S THEIR HARD LUCK! WHEN I SAY START— YOU START!
THE SOONER WE GET THIS STUPID PROCESSION OVER, THE SOONER I'LL BE WITH THAT DISHY JEREMY RINGMER I GOT DADDY TO INVITE DOWN FROM TOWN TO HAND OUT THE PRIZES!
AND SO THE PAGEANT GOT UNDER WAY...
AND BY THE TIME ROBIN HOOD AND HIS MERRY MEN ARRIVED...
SORRY, MISS SINDY! IT WAS MORE THAN MY JOB'S WORTH TO STOP HER!
START THE MUSIC AND THE DANCING! WE'RE NOT BEATEN YET!
HEY! THE PROCESSION ISN'T OVER YET! LISTEN TO THAT BEAT!

AREN'T THEY FANTASTIC?
IF YOU WANT TO JOIN IN THE DANCING YOU'RI WELCOME TO!

"GOOD QUEEN BESS" GAVE A REGAL WAVE AS SHE PASSED THE JUDGES' STAND...
HE ISN'T EVEN LOOKING!

BUT LOOK THE CELEBRITY DID, WHEN SINDY AND HER BROWNIES ARRIVED...
HEY, SINDY! I BET YOU'RE RESPONSIBLE FOR THIS LOT!
THAT YOUNG LADY HAS BEEN RESPONSIBLE FOR MOST OF THE PAGEANT!

TO SINDY WENT THE FIRST PRIZE, A VERY EXPENSIVE VIDEO AND MUSIC CENTRE WHICH SHE HANDED STRAIGHT OVER TO HER BROWNIE COMPANIONS...

AND WHAT HISTORICAL FIGURE DO YOU REPRESENT, YOUNG LADY?

I'M MARIAN'S MAID, SIR! MAID MARIAN IS MY BIG SISTER!

AND A PRETTY SISTER SHE IS, TOO! I RECKON YOU DESERVE THESE FOR BEING THE MOST ORIGINAL HISTORICAL CHARACTER!

COO! THE TWO HOLIDAY TICKETS! NOW MUM AND DAD CAN GO AWAY!

"GOOD QUEEN BESS" DID NOT EVEN GET A LOOK IN. THE REST OF THE PRIZES WENT TO THOSE WHO HAD MADE THEIR OWN COSTUMES...
HARD CHEESE, THELMA! IT DOESN'T LOOK AS IF WE'RE AMONGST THE PRIZES!
WHO CARES ABOUT STUPID PRIZES? IT'S JEREMY RINGMER I'M INTERESTED IN! IT'S TIME I INTRODUCED MYSELF!
HELLO, JEREMY! I'M SURE YOU KNOW WHO I AM!
WELL IN THAT COSTUME IT'S NOT DIFFICULT...
... I DON'T EVEN HAVE TO GUESS. YOU'RE GOOD QUEEN BESS!
...AND HE WENT BACK TO TALKING TO 'MAID MARIAN'.
PAH! HE HARDLY GAVE ME A GLANCE!
OH, NEVER MIND, THELMA! THERE'S STILL LITTLE ME!
THELMA!
I EXPECT SHE IS UPSET FOR GOING TO A WHOLE LOT OF TROUBLE FOR NOTHING!
SHE CERTAINLY DID, JILLY!